Broken Souls

Broken Souls

Finding God in the Silence of Suffering

Stefan Johnsson

ISBN: 979-8-9996093-0-4

All images, both the cover art and internal drawings were created by using ChatGPT through the Image Generator Pro application.

*This book is for all who have, who are, or who
will be struggling through a difficult time in
their life. Jesus is always the light at the end of
the tunnel, as long as you look for Him.*

Chapters

Introduction 1

The (Im)Perfect Armor 7

The Coffin 11

The Joy Found in Sadness 14

This Helpless Soul of Mine 16

Life, Loss, Lucy..18

God's Throne Room 21

The House (Part 1) – Moving In...25

The Knock 31

The End of the Rope..35

Warfare..38

The Accused 43

The Desert 48

To Touch the Edge of His Cloak...51

Forgiveness in Repentance 56

The House (Part 2) – The Living Room 58

Taking out the Trash..63

The Forest..66

Adrift 70

The Punching Bag 74

Forsaken and Forgotten 78

The Banquet 82

The House (Part 3) – The Private Office 88

The Irony of Success 93

Job's Lament 97

The Cloud 100

The Beach 105

Unstable Ground 108

The Panic Attack 112

Weak and Helpless 116

The House (Part 4) – The Bedroom 118

The Giant Shadow 125

A Second Chance 130

The Double-Edged Sword 135

The Betrayer 138

A Prayer to God 141

My Daughter 144

The Shower 148

The Millstone 152

No Greater Sin 156

The Anxious Heart 158

The House (Part 5) – The Basement 161

The Empty Bottle 166

Rock Bottom 170

The Glock 174

Give Up 177

Until Death 180

True Character...184

Finding Inner Tranquility 186

Sprinting Towards the Goal 188

My Devotion..190

INTRODUCTION

It's hard to give this book a true starting point. Throughout my life, I've used words to express emotions and pain that life has sent my way. These words became my outlet to try and understand pain and heartache while also remembering who I am and whose I am in Christ. I am able to, through words, express any situation or experience that I'm going through in life. This is how I survived as a young teenager, trying to transition into a new culture and lifestyle as my parents moved across the Atlantic Ocean.

So off and on I would write to help me release the tensions and emotions building up inside of me while creating an outer wall of protection from others. It was sometime later in my early 20s that I began to write on a blog and share poems and thoughts that I had on God or my experiences in life. God had healed me from my earlier years, but the writing remained as an outlet. One of the first stories that came from this period of time was *The (Im)Perfect Armor* that I wrote in 2010 when serving in a full-time ministry with at-risk teenagers.

When I started to settle down with a full-time job after completing my master's degree a couple years later, I found myself writing a lot more than before. It was in the years between 2014 and 2015 that I truly began building the foundations for *Broken Souls* without having any knowledge that some of these blog entries would eventually turn into a book. In January, 2025, I wrote the first draft of the chapter called *The Anxious Heart.* As I shared this story on social media, I wrote the following:

> *"I wrote this in response to the struggles I've had in my life. There [have] been many times where I did not have an answer to why I felt the way I did. I wanted to share this to those who are or will struggle through something. I am thankful for my family and the fellow Christian brothers in my life that have helped me through. There is no need to be alone in struggles and we all have them. I used 2 Corinthians 4:7-12 as a basis for this [short story]."*

When reflecting on these words, I find them to be true even today. And this has become the underlying reason behind *Broken Souls*.

We all struggle and go through so much heartache in life and no matter what we are told or read, the experience itself is no less real and painful. Emotions overcome reason. Jesus said in John 16:33, that we will have trials and sorrows but to take heart because He conquered the world. Then Paul writes in Romans 12:12 that we are to "rejoice in hope, be patient in tribulation, be constant in prayer." The hope is what Jesus did on the cross; patience is for knowing that tribulation will happen and there's no quick way to end it; and, prayer is for us to stay in communion with God through all that we are going through. Notice that nowhere does it promise or say that there is a quick healing to make the pain go away, the Bible only shares with us that it takes time and to lean on Jesus through it all.

One experience I will never forget was in the summer of 2016. I was going through a very difficult situation emotionally and I still decided to go on this trip that was planned since the start of the year. I wanted to be left alone on the plane flight, but God had something different waiting. A Jewish woman sitting next to me wanted to talk and I didn't, but her persistence ended up sparking a conversation that took the entire 2-hour flight. I ended up sharing my personal testimony, how important Jesus was to me, and how He had changed my life. It showed me that no matter how broken we are at certain times, the foundation of Christ is the rock that never falters or moves. God uses us when we are at our weakest, so that we know it is His strength that will carry us through any difficulty we may face in life.

Yet, many of us try to hide our pain and sorrows and try to deal with them on our own. We become distrustful and are afraid to be hurt even more which stops us from sharing our grief with others. It is easier to put on a smile in public or at church without asking for prayer, telling others that we are happy when we are not. But for those who do share their pain in safe spaces, there is a sense of healing, peace, and comfort. And on the other side of this, as someone who prays for others, the burden of carrying the pain of others and praying for them is rewarding, but also a sacrifice that is happily taken on.

Paul, in 2 Corinthians 1:3-4, speaks on how sharing in sufferings will help in times when others may also experience these same sufferings later. It brings comfort knowing that we do not have unique sufferings, and that others have gone through them before us. Then, in turn, these people can help us in our trials which allows us to continue this cycle of help for those who come after. It's how we bond and grow as a community of believers.

In 2018, I began to write a series on what I called *The House*. It had four parts to it, and it was the most read blog post that I shared at that time. The idea came to me when I read through *Mere Christianity* earlier that year. C.S. Lewis wanted to explain how God changes our lives and used an example of God moving into your house and creating a mansion. This concept really stuck with me, so I began to write a version of this using a fictional character. In October 2018, I posted part 3 (part 4 in this book) related to the bedroom. It wasn't using my own experiences, but from bringing together stories shared by friends or acquaintances. I realized then that what I'm writing would work much better in a book form. So instead of publishing part 4(part 5 in the book), I decided to grab many of the initial set of blog posts I had written up to that point in time and make it into the first outline of a book. It was barely over 20 stories or poems and many were replaced in this final draft, but it gave me a springboard to begin writing other stories.

Most of the original works that came before 2019, besides the ones already mentioned, included *God's Throne Room*, *Sprinting Towards the Goal*, *To Touch the Edge of His Cloak*, *The Doubled-Edged Sword*, and *The Cloud*. The rest have been written somewhere between 2018 and 2024.

As you go through the short stories and poems, you will notice that some are taken from verses in the Bible while most of the rest have been from various experiences or ideas that came to my mind. I wouldn't consider any story to be directly related to someone I know or a specific scenario, but the initial inspiration or concept may have come from a personal experience or interaction. For example, the story called "The Shower," came to me while taking a shower because I would use this place to think and dwell. Though, if you notice the final story had nothing to do with me, but only had the idea of what a shower may be for someone who is experiencing a very challenging and abusive life.

I do want to share that the story called, *Life, Loss, Lucy*, was originally written by a friend whose mother passed away. I asked for his permission to take the story and include it in my book, which he agreed. It was too powerful to exclude as it was based on real world sorrow. It has been edited some, but I tried my best to keep as much of the originality as I could. Personal experiences have a sense of connecting with others that fiction may not.

This book may not bring you joy to read, but that was not my intention. It is to remind us that there is always a light, a way out of the darkness that we may find ourselves in if we just trust in Jesus. This book should bring hope, that in your darkest days and the trials you may face, you are not alone. It took a lot out of me emotionally to write these stories, but my prayer and hope is that there is at least one person for each story who will find a connection and be comforted as they read through it. God meets us no matter where we are in life and the experiences we go through.

Stories are somewhat grouped by the flow of the short story sections for *The House*. Though, you cannot fully group all stories like this, so it is only meant to give some type of flow to the book. If you are reading this introduction to get some sense of what is in *Broken Souls*, I would say that my best advice is don't read through this book quickly. It is meant for deep reflection and thought. You may not feel a connection to each story, which is okay. Though, it is good to know that others may be struggling through a dark place that fits the story you read. It may also help you understand the trials of others more and help you emphasize with those who are hurting.

My prayer is that lives will be changed and hope restored for anyone that this book touches. My heart and soul are poured into these chapters, yet, I feel privileged that God gave me the creativity and inspiration to write the chapters and stories that are within. It was truly because of Him that this book was even able to be written and completed.

With that said, let the stories and poems within, that are inspired by God, reach your heart and soul and that you will be comforted in your trials and sorrows.

I have said these things to you, that in me you may have
peace. In the world you will have tribulation. But take heart; I
have overcome the world.
-John 16:33

THE (IM)PERFECT ARMOR

*Put on the whole armor of God, that you may be able to stand
against the schemes of the devil.*
-Ephesians 6:11

I stand broken and humbled by the pain and suffering that surrounds me. The tribulations in my life that should have left me beaten and bruised has somehow made me stronger than before. I gaze at the armor that protects me and I am in unbelief. There is not one piece that looks unbroken or viable, not one piece that should be protecting me anymore, yet it still does. Tears stream down my face as I remember that it was God who allowed me to choose my own path and it was Him who held me up and protected me when I saw my sin for what it was.

The belt of truth is torn and loose. Yet, it still surrounds my waist and keeps the rest of my armor from falling to the ground. Its imperfection lies in the countless times where I didn't look to God for truth. It was in worldly truth, truth based on lies and what my itching ears wanted to hear. I was led astray by my own sinful desires and deceived by empty promises of happiness and prosperity. I still fail to stand strong in God's Word, but he constantly reminds me of how His grace is sufficient, that I am saved by no means of my own, and that His love for me will never end.

The breastplate of righteousness lies in ruins, barely hanging on by a strap. It has been broken by the countless lies and different masks that I put on around others. I am ashamed by the need to hide my true identity and the peer pressure to follow the popular crowd. I want to live a life dedicated to God's Word, but I flee from persecution instead, quietly hiding my shame around other Christians. I

falsely carry the cross as I am more focused about what others see than what God sees. Yet, somehow, I am still protected as he forgives me and still loves me the same.

The sores on my feet are visible through the straps of the sandals. The pain from the dried blood and torn blisters reminds me of how I wanted to walk my own path rather than God's. Each time that I walked my own way I was hurt and broken, brought to my knees through the pain that I caused myself and others. Yet God's guiding hand kept bringing me back to the path he has set for me, gently applying salve and putting the sandals back on my feet. It is when I am on God's path that I find joy, happiness, and friendship which I lacked when I decided to walk alone and left God behind.

My shield of faith is that of a small buckler, barely covering my arm. My faith seems weak and shallow, letting the devils' arrows fly through unabated. Satan grabs me and pulls me away as my faith is not steadfast. But it was God's guiding hand that would not let me go, still saying that I am his for all eternity. Thanks be to God, for his faith in me never stops, even though my own falters with every arrow from Satan. He knows my limits and all he wanted was for my trust in him to carry me through.

The helmet of salvation is covered with dents, yet it still remains the strongest piece of my ragged armor. Even if everything in my life brings me down to my lowest point, the helmet never leaves my head. The helmet is God's promise that he will not break. It is the sign of his unconditional love for me. Even when I doubt, I still feel the helmet covering me. My life is safe thanks to God's love for me. He saved me and he will never let me go.

My sword drags on the ground as I barely have the power to lift it up on my own. Its edge is dull and the weight is heavy. I don't use the strength from God to lift it, and I don't use his words to sharpen it. Yet, God still guides me and gives me wisdom to make it through each day and for His will to be done. I find that the sword is the sharpest when I'm at my weakest and I have to lean fully on God. It is God who knows how to reach the hearts of people, not me. It is His Words and His Holy Spirit that sharpens my sword, not my own wisdom and will power.

I stand broken yet full of hope and surrounded by God's love. I am far from being a perfect soldier, but that is not what God asked me to be. He uses me as I am, sinful and imperfect. The war that is waged against the principalities of this world is there to make me lean on His strength and not my own. Even though I see my armor full of dents and holes, God does not. His perfect will is the real armor that allows me to stand strong. His love holds me up through the trials and temptations which stops me from following him completely.

Thank You Father, my God, my Lord, my shield and provider, for loving me through my weaknesses. Amen.

THE COFFIN

Silence filled the auditorium of the old church as the last few guests left through the closing doors. The sun's light reflected through the painted windows, creating a steady stream of lively colors in an otherwise somber moment of time. I stood still in the middle of the aisle, facing the inevitable finality that death had brought to my father. Tears would not come to my beck and call, but only a numb feeling which had settled over my soul. There was no blueprint that could tell me how I should feel or what mourning looked like. All I had were my own thoughts that swirled through my mind, keeping closed the doors of my emotions, refusing to blend the two together.

I wanted to see him one last time, to stand face to face with the man whose blood flowed through my veins. Yet, this immovable and gripping fear would not let me move forward. It was as if the mental block had shut me off from experiencing the pain that may come from such an encounter and was unwilling to open and let me through. It kept a vigilant guard over my movements and the emotional consequences that seeing my father would bring.

I was paralyzed from head to toe, standing still with only the sound of my breathing giving me a sense of control.

How could I move forward?

Should I move forward?

Was it worth it to see my father's emotionless face one last time?

Questions filled my mind as I thought about my father and his legacy. What did he leave me but failures of parenthood? Anger seeped its way through as I remembered how he was too busy for me and never seemed to care about my successes or dreams.

How could he fix this now?

There would be no apologies, no remorse that he could give me from the silence that death had brought. I had to move forward and learn to forgive a man who could not ask for it and may never have.

Did he even know the pain he caused?

I would get no answer. I do not know if the question itself angered me more or if it was that I would be left without a reply.

Was there any good in this man?

This father of mine left the living too quickly and too early. Anger had no use now as the coffin lay still in front of me. There was a long, drawn-out sigh coming from deep inside and the anger which had resided there began dissipating throughout the stagnant air around me. He was still my father and there would be no one else to replace him. He was a man who loved me in the best way he knew how, or so my mother constantly tried to tell me. Her wisdom had showed me that perfection could not be achieved, and his faults should not define his life or mine.

Failures will happen and the pain of these failures stay with the living while the dead move on.

I tried to see the goodness in my father and to see him for who he was. Deep down there was a part of me which believed he loved me in his own way. But this was not enough to let my emotions find an escape through the barriers of my thoughts.

Yet, facing him was not an easy task to complete.

He was no longer part of this world and memories of him would slowly fade and disappear. Few stories would remain over time to be shared with my children as life continued its never-ending cycle. But a part of him remained in me, his thoughts and actions that helped define who I had become, for good or bad. It was this that I would carry with me and pass on to the next generation. How I lived my life and treated those whom I love would be a reflection on him.

My father's legacy was me.

The question that remained would be what part of him I would carry on.

I turned to walk away from the man who had given me so much in life. Facing him was too much and something that I could not handle at this moment in time. Holding the door to the auditorium, I looked back one last time. I breathed out slowly to release the tension that had not yet left my body. Maybe someday I could face him with the door to my emotions wide open, but it would not be today, not while he lay in his coffin.

As I pulled open the door, I let my thoughts fade away into a place where it would remain, keeping the door to my emotions untouched and unopened. Today was not my day for mourning. But it would come, this I knew.

THE JOY FOUND IN SADNESS

It is better to go to the house of mourning
than to go to the house of feasting,
for this is the end of all mankind,
and the living will lay it to heart.
Sorrow is better than laughter,
for by sadness of face the heart is made glad.
-Ecclesiastes 7:2-3a

It is much worse to find yourself in the place of feasting,
Feeding the heart with noise, laughter, and everything pleasing.
The beauty of life does not grow but fades within, leaving only dust,
Memories on the hurt caused to others are lost in playful lust.
There is no time to stop and let sadness in to provide healing,
Creating a constant busyness where sorrow has no meaning,
It's the wisdom of fools that is heeded; friends are neglected, left out of sight,
Fading becomes life as in the coming of dusk, engulfing the power of the light.

It is much better to find yourself in the place of sorrow,
Feeding the heart with humbleness and reflection for tomorrow.
The broken heart speaks to the need for forgiveness, grace, and dependence,
In the solemn silence, the words echo in the halls of repentance.
The chisel can be heard, removing the rough edges of the living heart,
The ugliness left by a past full of pride and anger are torn apart.
It is what the soul needs, rising above the ashes of death and despair,
And joy fills life as in the coming of dawn, where darkness does not ensnare.

THIS HELPLESS SOUL OF MINE

Oh wretched, oh helpless soul of mine
How could I be so blind and not see the sign
All I could think of was my hurt and my pain
Unwilling to see beyond what I could gain

The justice that I sought, they had to pay
I sat down, thinking of what I would say
My mind was wrapped in a dark and thick cloud
I was too stubborn to realize, a bit too proud

Then my heart was touched by the God above
Descending on me like a perfect, angelic dove
I saw the pain in the Son who was so caring,
So loving, so kind, so gentle and caring

I begged my Savior, my Lord for help
To save this broken, selfish whelp
His compassion, his mercy, he showed to me
Providing a way to repent and finally be free

LIFE, LOSS, LUCY

My Dear Lucy,

If you can see what I write, please listen. If you can hear my cry, please respond. I need you to know, I need you to listen to my heart's plea. It is the last words I have the strength to write.

How close we were. A mother so faithful, a mother so kind, a mother so humble. Your courage in life gave me hope, your selfless care provided my sustenance. I breathed in life because of your sacrifice and the love you had for me.

I was, no…I am broken with scars from a life of pain and mistakes. Yet, you always believed the best in me, hoping and praying that I will be the person you always wanted me to be.

I was on my way there, I know, I was pulling myself back together. I thought that you would make it through whatever you were suffering and that it would allow me to do the same. God failed you and now I also believe that God has failed me. Why did you have to leave me in the worst possible way?

Losing you is the end of me.

How could you say that God would use you to save me? This can't be right. He must have abused your faith and played me like a violin. I feel that it was the complete opposite that came true. Isn't strong faith supposed to move mountains? Nay! It did not do so in this case, so why should I believe God's promises?

You left me too early and I do not know how to live this life without you. How can I have faith in a God that has let you leave this life too early? You were the pillar of faith for me and now you're gone. I miss you greatly, and I love you.

Dear God,

If you are listening to me. How can I embrace you now? My mother's faith in you was to the extreme and yet, she is the one that has left this earth. I've had enough of the promises that go unfulfilled and the love that you say you have for us. This pain is too real, and you could've ended it by saving Lucy from death. Yet, she is gone, and I am here.

I have never in my life questioned faith as much as I do now. What is the point of all this suffering and pain? It leads to nowhere except misery and emptiness.

If I am the one who lacks in faith and is living for myself, then why was I not taken instead? It is unfair and unjust. Lucy must be in peace with the angles because the opposite is unbearable. That is the least you could do for her. Her life on this earth was too short and you know it. So why, why was she taken away?

I will not pray to you again. Not now, not ever. I only give you one chance to show me that you have a reason for the pain, and then I shall repent. Let me know my mom did not die in vain. If so, I will change my ways and follow you.

Tell her that I love and miss her.

Sincerely,
A Broken Soul

GOD'S THRONE ROOM

I saw the Lord sitting upon a throne, high and lifted up;
and the train of his robe filled the temple.
Above him stood the seraphim.
And one called to another and said:
"Holy, holy, holy is the Lord of hosts;
the whole earth is full of his glory!"
And I said: "Woe is me! For I am lost;
for I am a man of unclean lips.
-Isaiah 6:1-3,5

"Holy, Holy, Holy!"

The words echoed in my head, louder and louder, until it became unbearable. How could I, a mere mortal, be kneeling in the throne room of the Almighty God, the Maker of heaven and earth, the Alpha and Omega, the Beginning and the End. I should have been in awe, but that was a fleeting thought. Nothing in me inspired praise for God at this moment in time.

"Holy, Holy, Holy!"

"Noooooo!" I cried out. I covered my ears in a fleeting attempt to drown the voices of the angels. I... am... not...worthy. There was no purity within me, my clothes were dirty and ragged compared to the shining white robes of the heavenly hosts surrounding the throne. My sin was laid bare...all I had done flowed like a rushing river through my mind, reminding me of how unholy, how broken, how selfish, and how conceited I had been. I wanted to disappear, to fall through the floor, to forget where I was. I sought darkness, a sanctuary away from God's

judgment. I would give my life for this, anything rather than His throne room, this place of holiness.

"Holy, Holy, Holy!"

It was too much to take. Tears filled my eyes, dripping on to the floor as it marred the reflection of myself – a perfect metaphor for the imperfections of my soul. I had to disappear, to forget my wrongs, my faults, and my sin. All I could do was try and make myself as small as I
could, hoping that the floor would swallow me up. But the stones refused to obey my commands as it was a strong foundation that could not be moved.

"Holy, Holy, Holy!"

I was overcome with sorrow and grief for all I had done wrong. I pulled at my hair in a vain attempt to remove the memories flooding through my mind. All my life I had thought that I was good enough, better than the other people who lived in my community. But not until I was in the presence of God did I realize how badly I missed the mark, how unholy I truly was. The darkness inside overwhelmed me.

"Holy, Holy, Holy!"

"I know!", I cried with a half-hearted attempt to quiet the angels. I understand, there is nothing that I could do to fix what I had done. All that I was left with was my memories and pain. I deserve the judgment, the punishment.

"Please," I begged, "send me away, let me pay for my sins." There is nothing more righteous, nothing more deserving of justice than condemning me for all I have done.

"Holy, Holy, Holy!"

The words increased in strength, but I was spent. I had nothing left but sorrow. Dejected and humbled, I could only wait for the verdict, the decree from God.

"Holy, Holy, Holy!"

In my emptiness, where I could fall no lower, I felt a warmth, a gentle hand on my shoulder. As I watched in astonishment, I could see my clothes turning white, removing all the shame and sin which had covered my body. A feeling of freedom, a cleansing was being done from within. I knew it, I knew it was Jesus

Himself. He took my sin from me, the thoughts, the deeds in my mind. They began to feel as a distant memory, a past life that was no longer part of who I am.

He whispered to me, "I paid the price for your sins. I bought the debt. I took it upon myself so that you can be free."

"I know," I said, "but I don't feel like I deserve it."

"It was not your choice to make. I did it out of love. Now go, sin no more. Tell others the good news," Jesus replied. And with a powerful voice, He added, "I will be with you."

As I opened my eyes, the feeling of warmth remained. I realized that I could not live my life in grief any longer and the condemnation began to fade. Jesus took it away and I was here to live my life for Him. I knew He was with me, to change me from the inside each and every day. A smile began to slowly cover my face.

The echoes of the angels could still be heard in my head, as they sang in worship, "Holy...holy....holy, is the Lord God Almighty!"

THE HOUSE (PART 1) – MOVING IN

"Imagine yourself as a living house. God comes in to rebuild that house. At first, perhaps, you can understand what He is doing. He is getting the drains right and stopping the leaks in the roof and so on: you knew that those jobs needed doing and so you are not surprised. But presently He starts knocking the house about in a way that hurts abominably and does not seem to make sense. What on earth is He up to? The explanation is that He is building quite a different house from the one you thought of ...He is building a palace. He intends to come and live in it Himself."
-C.S. Lewis, Excerpt from *Mere Christianity*

I always believed that the choices I made in my life wouldn't haunt me in the end, that there was nothing after death or a god to hold me responsible. Though, this was the worst kind of illusion. Each decision, each choice I made took me down a deeper and darker path of despair. It started with a barely noticeable slope, nothing too steep or slippery, and going down was as easy as...walking. The accumulation of the miles walked led me to the inevitable place, a basement, a place that I perceived as the bottom of the worst part of hell. The sorrows, the fear, the pain, and the heartache had made me a shadow of my former self. I do not remember if there was just one thing or one event which had led me to where I was, but there could not be a way out or redemption for a person such as me...or so I believed.

Had it not been for that one friend in my life, I would have been stuck in this wretched place forever. He was that one individual who never let me go and who gave off a light which caused the darkness to run away. He had given me hope where there was none and strength when I was too weak. All he kept telling me was that I needed to accept the free gift of salvation found in Jesus and that the grace of God will give me a new life.

"I way out?" It can't be real I thought to myself. Yet, when I looked around me, I realized that I had nothing to lose, so I grasped onto this hope with all my remaining strength, closed my eyes and waited...for something. I asked for God to rescue me and lift me out of this wretched place, this darkness that seemed like a fairytale in itself. The seconds ticked by in what seemed like eternity. Then the unexpected happened. I felt as if I was being dragged out from my own hell so fast as if someone had put me on an elevator to the top of the tallest building. You know, like the ones that make you feel as if you are shooting up into the clouds at the speed of light.

The path I took to accept Jesus into my life brought so much joy and love which I had never experienced before. I was a new man and forever changed. At first, butterflies filled my stomach as I knew that my life would be different and better, but I had no idea what to expect. Part of the deal, which at first made no sense to me, was that Jesus said he was going to come and move into my house. What kind of deal was this, I thought? Couldn't he just stay in His place up in the sky, and I could just call on Him whenever something went wrong? I thought that was what He did; how He rescued us and waited for the next time we needed help. Well, no matter how weird it seemed at first, I had made the decision to follow Him, so if this was part of the deal, then why not give it a try? After all, I was a free man for the first time in my life. Freed from the horrible darkness and the shackles of sin that had brought me to my lowest point.

Time slowly went by as I anxiously waited for my new guest to arrive. It was the first time anyone would stay for even one night at my house. I felt proud of my cleaning. Any clothes lying around were tossed into a neat pile, hidden within my closet. My shoes were not in order, but all of them were stacked to the side, making it easy to walk into the house without tripping. I had done my best to vacuum, at least around the furniture. No point to move them. Even the bathroom felt clean for once as the most basic stains were wiped with some paper towels and water. It was more than the usual whenever a close friend dropped by to visit. I was proud of my work and smiling ear to ear, knowing that any guest would feel that my house was clean enough and livable.

I expected Jesus would bring with him what he needed for moving in, but as I saw him walking towards my house from a distance, all I could see was…him. There was no baggage, no moving truck, and no possessions of any kind. Who was this man? He seemed to come without any concern for the material things that this world requires to live. He must at least have a cellphone – an essential item needed for anyone in this world – because how else would he be able to connect with all his friends? Well, if he wanted one, or anything else for that matter, he would have to buy it himself. There was no way that I would let him use mine. I had very personal information that I wouldn't dare to share with anyone, much less him.

Here he was, ready to move in to my place, all smiles and welcoming, as if he had been waiting for years! He just ran up to me and gave me the biggest hug. If this was how nice he was in person, the deal of us living together will not be so bad after all I thought.

After some quick introductions, he began sharing his plans and purpose for being there. His ideas to help keep my house clean and cozy were well-intentioned, but he wanted access to the entire house. This I could not allow. For starters, my office, bedroom, and basement were off limits and only for me. He had no reason to go to these areas, as they were private and personal. I wanted to keep my spiritual and social lives separated, so he better be understanding of this now while we were first getting to know each other. The best scenario would be if he could take care of my house and keep it in order without getting in my way or into my personal business. It would look much better if a girl would come over, seeing the spotlessness of my house and not realizing Jesus was my roommate. A smile crept over my face, as I thought to myself, always show off my best side first because girls like that.

I enjoyed this new relationship throughout the honeymoon period, and I saw changes in my life that I liked. He fixed some of the rot in the wood and leaking

pipes in the drainage system. Though, that's where it ended. The worst part was that he never asked permission before throwing things away. I didn't realize it until I needed something, a pair of shoes here, or my favorite shirt there. When I found out what he was doing it was because my liquor cabinet was emptied and cleaned.

If he was going to drink it, he could have at least asked me first! So I confronted him about being an alcoholic and his thievery. Then, with a straight face, he told me he had thrown the bottles away, stating that it wasn't necessary for me to have because of how it led me into sin and fitful rages. I was boiling with anger! Well, if he wanted rage, then I'll show him my rage. Who throws out good liquor?! I wanted to kick him out. All that money, all that vintage alcohol…gone! We got into a screaming match, well, okay, I admit, it was only me screaming, but I felt justified for it. I asked him about other things that had gone missing and he had the audaciousness to admit putting it all in the garbage. He obviously had a poor way of defining what garbage was. This was crossing the line for me. There was no respect for my possessions or my house!

"I've had enough! Out my house!" I yelled. "This is my life and you do not have the right to tell me what to do!" I seethed with rage and walked into my room, shutting the door with a resounding boom. He better be gone by the time I came back downstairs I told myself. The anger reminded me of who I was before I met Jesus and how upset I would get when I did not get my way or when someone did something I didn't like. This deal was starting to suck, and I did not like it one bit. As if I would allow Jesus to get his own way? Why couldn't I just have fun and do what I wanted in my life? Every piece I collected from my past is part of me and I did not want to let it go. It was what allowed me to have fun. How could I just...leave it all behind?

I tossed and turned in my bed and soon gave up, staring at the ceiling. The initial shock and anger wore off, but my thoughts kept me awake. I started to remember the things he had thrown away. The pair of shoes from a previous job where I had cheated the company out of thousands of dollars for personal gain before quitting. The shirt I had for when I would go out to clubs and pick up girls for one-night stands. They liked how it looked and my confidence lacked without it. The liquor came from my special cabinet where I would go to grab several shots when I was the most depressed and wanted to drink my sorrows away. Lacking these things seemed bad at first, but I did not really miss them as much as I thought. Did I need them? I wanted them, but all these things which gave me happiness, it only lasted for a short while before I felt even worse afterwards. Peace, that feeling of contentment, only came whenever I was around Jesus, but never without him.

Ahhhh!! The man that I kicked out of my house was starting to make me second guess myself. He must've poisoned my mind, making me all forgiving and such. I started to dislike this feeling when I wanted to act out, but couldn't. I knew Jesus' intentions were for my best and that he was right, though, why did it have to be the stuff that I liked the most which he threw out? Maybe he just did not understand what he should or should not touch.

I left my room and walked downstairs. In a way, I was shocked to see him sitting quietly at the kitchen table, but also relieved he hadn't left. I guess he was just waiting for me to apologize for my behavior. I still expressed my clear disapproval of his actions as he had not asked me first, but I did, reluctantly, apologize to him for my behavior in the end. "You can stay," I told him, "Just ask me first before throwing something away." He only smiled back and told me that he was here to help me put my life on the right track. Wasn't it already on the right track? Either way, I thought, I had to keep an eye on this Jesus more than before. At least the most important items were locked in my personal rooms. But for now, maybe I should try to get to know Jesus a little more and find some way for us to connect.

THE KNOCK

*Behold, I stand at the door and knock. If anyone hears my voice
and opens the door, I will come in to him and eat with him, and
he with me.*
-Revelation 3:20

"Leave me alone!" I screamed out loud, hoping that the person on the other side of the door would hear me. But the knocking was like clockwork, always consistent, never late.

Unstoppable. Unchanged. Unperturbed.

Who would keep knocking on my door like that? I was very clear, to myself, that this door would never be opened. The question was when the other person would finally realize this and go away. Nothing could convince me to give in and open this door. Getting up would mean letting go of my pride and admit humility, a character trait that would admit defeat.

Even still, the constant noise kept me from focusing on what I wanted to do. It was a continuous nagging in the back of my head that refused to go away. I could go on with my day, but the moment I got home, sat down, let the quietness come in, the knocking would begin. It was, as if, the person knew when the best time to knock would be.

"Leave me alone!" I screamed at the top of my lungs. The sound cut into the silence of the house, and as the quietness settled back in, the knocks on the door began anew.

The consistent noise kept me from dwelling on my loneliness. Any reflection on my life would often come with thoughts of failure, mistakes, and the lack of

satisfaction that this world continuously brought. The knocks always interrupted me when I was deep in these thoughts, and I would rather prefer to keep my time of sorrow than hearing this noise.

Why then, I asked myself, would the knocks only come when I was feeling lonely and depressed? Did it promise to bring me a solution to this solitary life of mine? Did this person believe they could fill the void in my heart that nothing had ever accomplished before? Truth couldn't exist. This world was too dark to provide any light or redemption for my depression.

Yet, the knocks continued with no end. It was a persistent calling to be answered. Maybe, just maybe, I could go and find out who this person knocking really was? I could give him a piece of my mind. What did I have to lose?

I sensed a bit of my pride give way, or maybe it was just replaced by curiosity? Either way, it gave me the shivers. It was a foreign thought that hadn't occurred to me before, and I didn't know how it got there.

The thought came to my mind again and felt stronger than before. What if I opened this door and then told the person to stop knocking, and it would all be over? Would this person try to fix my life? If so, I definitely didn't need a therapist, and I definitely didn't need someone to tell me what I had to do. I've had these kinds of people try to help me before and no one could make me feel better beyond a week or two.

I could hear the rhythmic knocking continue, asking me to open the door. It must've been a strong wind that came through my house, but for some reason, I wasn't sitting anymore. This urge was guiding my movements as I was slowly walking towards the closed door.

Maybe my heart was defying my mind, and I couldn't tell what was truly guiding me.

Maybe it was this need to find the answer that I was looking for.

Maybe there was some hope left in me that someone could give the answer that I longed for.

The door loomed down the hallway and seemed more distant than it really was. I did not know if I had the courage to keeping walking, but my feet kept moving forward as if guided by a giant magnet. With each step, my heartbeat increased, the anticipation building to what I was about to do. I must have walked a marathon before reaching the door, but the hardest part was yet to come.

The handlebar felt smooth to the touch, and my nerves almost overwhelmed me. I knew, if I didn't do it now, I would never do it again. I slowly pushed down on the handle until it wouldn't go any further. I took a deep breath as I pulled the door open. A bright light starting to shine through, and I could see a figure in white standing before me. Whoever he was, I thought, he would change my life forever.

THE END OF THE ROPE

"Let go!" The persistent cries were carried by the swirling wind surrounding me. I couldn't tell how far below the distorted sounds were coming from and the darkness of the night didn't help. Yet, the words of encouragement did nothing more than remind me of the predicament I was in. They were on solid ground far below me, and not at the end of this rope. Could they even see where I was at? Did they not know that my very life was hanging by a simple thread? The fear of the unknown kept me from moving and every fiber of my being cried out to hold on.

I dangled at the end of the rope, holding on as if my life depended on it. My eyes strayed downward, looking into the emptiness that stretched on for what seemed like an eternity. The frizzled end of the rope hung just below my feet as it swayed in the wind. I had created a leverage point with my legs to keep my body stable and to preserve energy. I knew, deep down, that this temporary hold wouldn't last forever. A decision would have to be made soon. But how could I let go? I felt torn as I hugged the only other solid object I could see, believing that it would give me the strength to stay alive.

What a fool I had been to climb down the rope to begin with. My supposed friends, these "Christians," told me that this was the only option for eternal life. Believing that they cared for me I climbed down the rope, thinking that it would lead me to stable ground below, full of life, laughter, and leisure. They betrayed me by giving a false sense of hope. There was too much in this life that I still needed, and I had to hold on.

If only I could manage the strength to climb all the way back to the top. But I was too afraid to move and the screams to let go would not stop. Their words were a persistent annoying buzz that floated in the wind, but for some reason it brought comfort knowing that I wasn't alone. Yet, it didn't stop me from being upset in

believing them; that this hope of eternal life in Jesus would somehow rescue me from my sin. I looked up and without any stars to guide me, I could only see an empty darkness covering the path I had once taken to climb down. And this darkness above looked to be more ominous than what was below.

I began to think about what I had left behind. Not only was climbing up going to be near impossible, but I was not really sure I wanted to go back. The pain, the hurt, and the loneliness that the world offered had become too much to bear. I only sought out a church because of the joy that I had found in the people who had lived with an unexplained peace in their lives. As if they were unaffected and carefree from the world and its darkness. I just did not think that their solution to life would be to crawl down a hole to a place below with a rope that wasn't long enough to reach the bottom. It didn't take much imagination to understand what kind of death that a freefall would bring.

My head sunk into my shoulders. I began to feel defeated, wondering why this was the only option that I could find for the meaning of life. Was it just a moment of weakness that had led me down this path? What if I had looked for other options, other solutions before taking this one? All this required faith, and right now, there was very little to be had in my life. Letting go and believing meant putting my trust in Jesus. What if this was misplaced? The back and forth in my mind grew tiresome.

It was too late now, I thought, I had gone too far to not let go in faith. It was this nagging feeling I had in the back of my head, this mustard seed of faith, that somehow made me believe that this was the only truth that existed in the world. It felt real and honest even through the hesitancy that existed. It was the reason that I had first begun to descend. Why then could I not let go of this rope? The question lingered as I swayed in the wind.

It must've been a mental slip, but my legs untangled and the grip I had on the rope loosened. I struggled to regain my grip, but the rope slid through my hands. As I fell, the weight of the world began to grow lighter. Somehow, I knew this was not the end for me, but a chance for a new life and a new beginning. The bottom would be a soft and comfortable impact.

WARFARE

Fight the good fight of the faith.
-1 Timothy 6:12

The bullets flew overhead with increased velocity as the sounds pierced my ear drums, numbing out any other noise around. It all seemed to be happening in slow motion; wondering if it was a dream rather than the reality that surrounded me. The protective helmet did little to calm my fears, providing me an illusion of security. Yet, I held on to it as if it was the only thing that could save my life from the devastation coming down from above. Not a bone in my body had the courage or the want to get up and fight in the battle.

No one told me what the contract had entailed when I signed up. They all looked at me like it was the best decision I could make on earth, that my life would be better than it had been at any point before. I didn't truly believe it at first, but their happiness and joy made it seem so real and convincing. If this was what being a soldier in the army of God was like, then it cannot be that bad. So I did what any person in my place would've done, I signed on the dotted line. There was a party and celebration that came that day and it felt like things would only get better from that point forward. I was happy and full of joy by how everyone made me feel.

As the celebration died down, I found myself walking home well after midnight with the moon guiding my path. Sleep came quickly, carrying with it dreams of my future life and all the good times that would be coming my way. Life would truly be better with all the good things that were promised me.

Everything changed the moment a loud voice woke me up at the crack of dawn. I could barely orient myself, trying to figure out why my comfortable sleep was rudely interrupted. An army officer stood next to my bed, wetting my face with his spittle as he yelled for me to get dressed in short order. I was still in shock and groggy from the lack of sleep when he threw a uniform on top of me as if to say that my lateness was delaying him more than it should. I couldn't react at first as it all happened too fast, wondering what was going on and who this officer was. How did he even get into my house? I asked as much, and he avoided the questions. Instead he took out a piece of paper and asked me if this was my signature on the contract, which I couldn't deny. He said I would be going to the frontlines that day and the fighting couldn't wait for my questions or delays. My duty, he said, required my presence immediately. There would be no training, no boot camp, and no excuses. I was recruited into a war I had no intention to fight in.

What had I signed up for?

What battle would I be fighting?

Was this all a joke?

It all seemed like a horrible dream that I couldn't wake up from and had no end. Would I die the day after I was promised joy and happiness upon signing this contract? Why would anyone leave out that a war was being fought and that I had signed up to fight in it?

Throughout my life, I never thought or imagined to be part of any warfare. I only wanted peace and quiet, to experience comfort and relaxation, and enjoy the company of my friends. There was no reason to sacrifice all that to fight in a battle with my life at risk. Now I was being sent to the front lines where death seemed assured and the hope for a long life all but lost.

I was immediately put into the heat of battle and was scared more so than any other time in my life. I lay in the ditch, thinking back upon what happened, but it did not stop the reality of my current predicament. The war raged on all around me while I felt defeated, scared, and vulnerable. There was nothing in me that defined courage. My whole life was a disappointment of trying to please, trying to care, and tired of always falling short. I found contentment in just living without letting

others down. How the Commander of this army thought I could help I do not know. My inadequacies should have kept me from joining this war as I would've failed even the basic physical examination or mental health test. They had to have made a mistake to add me into their battle unit.

Maybe I was to be just another body that could be thrown into the fire. Maybe I would be used and discarded without a second thought. Could it be that I really was that insignificant and expendable to the commander of this army?

I put my head into the mud below. I wanted to be buried where I lay, to hide from the sounds of warfare above and not think about the lack of courage or shame that slipped into my mind. More than anything, I wanted to go home and back to my normal life. I had no courage, no strength to get up and try again. I pushed my hand into the mud, wanting to pull my body further down into the soil below.

It was at the moment of greatest despair that I heard the voice that I did not want to hear. "Get up!" he said. "I recruited you to fight!" The voice of the Commander pierced through the explosions and bullets around me. It was as if we were stuck in a time capsule where everything around us paused in anticipation of my answer.

His demand was something I could not give. Did he not know how much of a coward I really was? I was ready to run the opposite way, to desert everyone and give up rather than fight. What would he say if he truly knew all my thoughts? His face showed no anger or scorn. Nor did it
look like he would leave me alone or cast me out. Instead, he grabbed my shirt color and pulled me out of the trench with ease right as an explosion swept through the trench, consuming everything in its path. I quickly turned around and covered by face, thinking it was too late to move further away from the deadly flames. Instead, the commander's protection somehow held the flames back, and I could only feel the heat as it burned the air around my face. Only a few seconds had passed as the shock of what happened wore off.

I wanted to flee, but I knew there would be no bargaining with him, not after he had saved my life. His demands were simple and straightforward, yet required my everything. There would be no desertion. He turned to face me and all the words I wanted to say seemed to disappear before I could speak. It felt as if this commander knew everything about me and the fears that kept me from partaking in the battle.

He put His hand on my shoulder and said, "The trench is where the enemy finds its prey. Be strong and courageous for I am here with you." The warmth of His hand and the strength of His words came with such power that it seeped into my very bones. I felt renewed, full of vigor, and the fears beginning to slip away. The battle raged on, but somehow, I knew that taking part in the warfare above was safer than hiding in the trench below.

THE ACCUSED

My accusers sat close by with hatred in their eyes that burned with fire. Even as I tried to look away, I could feel their gazes cutting a hole through my very being. We all sat in silence within the courtroom, waiting for the judge to return so he could give his final verdict. The ticking of the clock mounted on the wall could be heard easily enough as it provided some semblance that time was moving forward. The wait felt like an eternity, but at least the trial was over, the evidence laid bare, and the decision imminent. Any hope for my innocence had been lost from the onset, and I knew that the outcome would be what was shown to be true all long.

Guilty.

I looked down at my feet as I sat in the hard, wooden chair. Who could dare to look at their accusers and feel any more shame than I already did?

The final sentence and the only punishment for my crimes was certain death. There was nothing I could say, nothing I could do to overcome the sin I had caused to those who had prosecuted me and brought me to this moment of time. The trial was fair, the evidence solid, and the judge had shown no partiality. It was crystal clear to me what the outcome would be. There were no more excuses or lies that could help me. Death was coming and the rest of my life, my hopes, and my dreams were forfeit. I was to be stoned to death and no one would come to my rescue.

My accusers knew my sin and the likely judgment to come. Crooked smiles formed on their lips as they enjoyed every last minute of my demise. It was they who would be throwing stones into my vulnerable flesh and executing the final judgment. It was justice for them and death for me. There was no other way to pay, no other way to make amends.

Blood had to be spilled.

I knew my life was one of imperfection, a flesh tainted by the sins of this world. I deserved the wrath to come, the death at the hands of my accusers. Stones would be cast and my life would be taken.

I wanted mercy, but I expected none.

The trial began upon my retirement as those who had accused me gathered evidence throughout my life, piece-by-piece and scrap-by-scrap, until their case was airtight. They stalked me, followed me, watched me, and waited for a time when the crimes committed were too high for me to find a way out. All of it, every last detail and misdeed was gathered and kept until the trial could be set. Their goal was simple; it was to see me fail so that the stones could be thrown. Who am I to stop them? Who am I to stand up against my accusers? Nay. I couldn't do that. Even if I had tried harder, there would still be things done that could be used against me. There was no way to escape them or their wrath. Perfection was unattainable and out of my reach.

My accusers couldn't accept anyone who tried to do good or looked better than they. It brought jealousy and rage, and it made them more aware of their own failures. Yet, there was nothing I could do to stop them. Throughout my life I knew that this time would come. It was inevitable, a final reading of my life for all in the courtroom to hear.

"All rise!" The sound of the bailiff caught me off guard and brought me back to the present. I slowly rose to my feet as the judge made his way to his chair. The conclusion to everything had finally come. I put my hands over my face briefly, imaging the stones that were to be thrown after the verdict was given.

"You may all be seated," the judge spoke. His tone showed fairness and compassion, something that helped me feel at ease in front of all my accusers. I lifted my head up, trying to show some final bit of courage before everything came crashing down to its ultimate conclusion.

"The evidence has been shown plainly for all to see, and you have plead guilty to these charges, yes?" The judge spoke with a firm voice while looking my way, ready to pronounce his judgment.

"That is correct, your honor." The reply barely escaped my lips, but little could be done now but to stand tall with my accusers looking on and the judge in front of me.

"Then I pronounce you guilty!" the judge made his verdict as he slammed his hammer on the wooded surface below. "The sentence for your crimes is death by stoning."

I couldn't take it anymore and sat back down in my chair and began to cry. The strength that was there for me during the sentencing had all gone away. My life was over and there was no mercy for a broken soul like me.

Cheers came from my accusers that sat next to me. All their work had not been in vain as their case against me was completed. They were ready for my funeral and couldn't wait to execute the final judgment.

Why me? Why did they not go after someone else? I felt broken and empty inside.

Before the bailiff could remove me, there was some whispers from the crowd. I didn't pay attention at first, but soon more people began to notice what was going on. Curiosity took hold of me, even with tears filling my eyes. I looked up and saw the judge standing next to me, his gown was off and he was covered in a simple white garment.

I couldn't believe what was happening. What was the judge doing so close to a sinner like me?

He looked in my eyes and I could see them filled with compassion and mercy. "I cannot take away your guilt," he said, "but I can take on your punishment for you and accept the death that your sins deserve."

I wiped my eyes with my sleeve and looked in wonder. In between sniffles, I replied, "you would do that for me? Why? I don't deserve mercy or the grace that you are giving me. I am as guilty as my accusers say that I am."

"You are guilty, that is true," he replied. "But I am willing to pay the price so you can go free. You are my child, and your guilt does not define who I see you to be. All you must do is accept the sacrifice that I am willing to give on your behalf."

I didn't believe it, at first. Why would someone love me so much to die in my place? It sounded so absurd, so crazy. But a part of me wanted to believe in this act of mercy. The courtroom had gone silent as everyone focused on me and the decision that was to be made. Either I refused the sacrifice by the man standing by my side or accept what he offered and watch him die in my place.

If this man knew what he wanted to do, why should I stop him? I pondered this for a few minutes, but believed that this was an authentic gesture and one that he was willing to give. I breathed out a sigh and then looked up at him and nodded my head. Words were hard to come by at that time, but I finally found the words to say, "I accept."

It was at that time the bailiff came to lead this man away, this judge before he stepped down from his bench.

My debt was wiped away, my guilt was gone, but how? I wanted to know more. It was all so new to me.

With rage in their eyes, my accusers cried to the judge for justice, but knew that there was nothing they could do. It was all over. No matter what mistakes that I would commit from now on could not be used against me. I was free, but they, they were still in pain and anger that could not be satiated. The guilty verdict was not enough for them. They wanted me dead.

I cried out to the judge who was being led out. "What about my accusers," I said. "What are to become of them?!"

He turned back and looked me in the eyes one last time. "Their time will come," he said. And with that he was gone through the side door and the courtroom began to empty. My accusers passed me by as they began to exit, but their haughty eyes didn't have the same effect on me as before. Their chance to see me dead was gone, and there was nothing that they could do about it. The verdict was fair and the price paid in blood.

A sense of peace overwhelmed me like nothing before. Chains were broken and freedom had been gained for the first time. A smile came to my face as I slowly made my way to the exit. I took one last look back at the courtroom and pictured the judge seated, resurrected and holy, and shining with a light beyond all imagination.

THE DESERT

The blurry shape of palm trees in the distance gave my eyes a chance to focus once more. I refused to believe, deep down, that this was just a hallucination. Too many times before my eyes had played tricks on me and I no longer knew what was true or not. My feet kept moving forward even though the anticipation of finding a place of tranquility was all but lost. It was either that or giving up and letting the desert sands take my soul away. My body's empty feeling of hope matched the energy that barely carried my footsteps over the next dune as I silently cried out for just a taste, a droplet of water on my parched lips.

The desert sand provided an unbearable heat that seeped through my soles as it succumbed to the hot sun from above. The sand clung to my body, burning, fighting for a chance to make its way further into my skin. No longer did I seek to remove it, I welcomed the pain as it gave me a sense that a small portion of life still remained within me. My body craved respite, a want of reprieve from the continuous fight for survival. Giving up felt like the right thing to do and my mind urged me to do so. Nothing within me wanted to go on and reach the blurry shapes that grew in the distance.

This sight, this hallucination in front of me may be the last lie that I would have to suffer through. My whole life was spent believing others who never cared to keep secrets or tell me the truth. Each lie that they told only cut me deeper inside. I was left unable to trust even those who had been closest to me.

It changed me from within, making me unable to share with others about the pain in my life and what I was going through. "Trust me," were words that never rang true and always meant the opposite. Secrets could no longer be shared and pain had to find itself a dark corner within my soul with a lock and a hidden key. I could only trust myself and no one else. It was a sad existence, a place of loneliness

and isolation which made me want to let the desert take my soul and envelop me into its shifting sands.

Forgotten was the way in which I had come and lost was the path that I was traveling. I had veered too far away into the desert sand, going my own way and unable to trust anyone for directions or help. Now I was truly alone where the sands had no end, no fulfillment, and no respite. All I craved was the living water to nourish my pained and forgotten soul. But I had lost my way and fallen victim to the lies radiating from the desert that I traveled in. If only I could have trusted someone, then maybe I would not be in this place of loneliness.

Too late, too far have I pushed myself away from others. No one could understand and see how undesirable I had become and the distrust in people had grown too vast, too deep for anything to mend it back together.

How could I ever begin to open my heart once more only to be hurt again by others?

No more would I withstand the lies and deceit. I wanted to cry out to someone for help, but they would only break my trust. It was inevitable; just like all those who had come before.

No medicine could ever heal what was already shattered and broken.

My voice had no power, no sound, no movement as the breath I gave carried with the wind that moved across the dunes. I was now part of the desert; my destiny and fate sealed for eternity. Alone I had ventured into this desert and alone I would succumb to it.

It was then that my heart reached out to God, a last hope, a last chance that maybe, just maybe his compassion would see through all the pain that kept me from crying out for help. Would his grace and mercy be what my heart longed for? If I could just taste his goodness before my last breath on this earth, then it would satisfy me. Just maybe I could put my trust in one last person, one last chance for redemption.

My eyes closed as I felt the energy leave my body with the final step I could muster. My knees buckled under the weight it had carried for so long. I imagined where life would have been with God and tried to dream of it before my body fell towards the earth below.

With a sudden shock, it wasn't the sand of the desert that finally stopped my fall. Instead it was the feeling of living water that splashed against my skin. It refreshed my soul and filled me with love and warmth that I had never experienced before. Yes, this feeling is what I had truly longed for my whole life. I knew now that I would make it through the desert. I wasn't alone anymore and never would be again.

TO TOUCH THE EDGE OF HIS CLOAK

*As Jesus went, the people pressed around him. And there was a
woman who had had a discharge of blood for twelve years, and
though she had spent all her living on physicians, she could not
be healed by anyone. She came up behind him and touched the
fringe of his garment, and immediately her discharge of blood
ceased.*
-Luke 8:42-44

Before I could process what was going on, pain wracked my body from the
inside out, burning from deep within my very soul. A whimper escaped my lips,
giving off a hopeless cry for help that would never come. Each gasp for air was a
constant struggle for survival and it took every bit of strength I had to fight through
the agony that would not let go.

I could never get used to the pain that spread throughout my body, causing
me daily suffering. No one could save me, and no healing possessed a magical
formula for the disease that sought my very life. All I had was gone and there were
no options left to bring me hope for a cure. As the pain subsided, my mind could
finally process what was going on around me.

There was something different about this noise that had awakened me so
suddenly. I could hear the crowd in the distance and my mind felt that it carried
with it something that I must have, a spark of hope that would bring life back to
my weak body. My cry for help fell on deaf ears, but still I tried. The house carried
the soundwaves throughout its empty rooms, unable to provide more than an echo

from its lifeless stones. I was on my own, but this would not stop me. Determination kept me from letting go of the life I lived.

The window above was low enough to reach. As I pulled myself up with the strength of both hands and clenched teeth, I began to see the beginnings of a crowd forming in the distance. The commotion was bringing a profound sense of excitement to the entire village that grew with each passing minute. It was hard to see it all from my second-floor window, but I knew that this was something more important than life itself.

A couple of the villagers came walking past and I cried out to them, hoping they would hear my voice. As they raised their heads, I gathered myself enough to ask who or what it was that caused the crowds to gather at the edge of town. Their surprise was evident, as if what I asked had been common knowledge to everyone around. "It's Jesus of Nazareth who is coming this way," one replied. "We want to see the miracles and hear the Rabbi speak for ourselves." As if this finished their duty with me, they quickly left towards the approaching crowd, not wanting to miss another minute of what Jesus would do or say.

I was left to my own thoughts. "Miracles?" I voiced out loud. Could He cure someone like me? I had to find out. I needed to find out. If only I could just get close enough, to be in His presence, then He may show me mercy.

I could see the crowd moving in my direction, as if they would be passing by my very house. The sounds of people and that calming voice…it's unmistakable. It has to be Him that I have heard so much about. The strain of pulling myself up to the window was hard enough and I let go and fell back down to my bed. I had to conserve my strength for what would come next. It would be my only chance, the only opportunity to change my life and heal that pain which had been with me for so long.

The Rabbi who heals the sick, the lame, the deaf, and the blind is coming my way, but not into my house. The hardest part was standing up without something to hold on to and my current goal was to reach the stairs that lay only a short distance in front of me. The first couple steps came quickly with a loss of balance. I fell forward, hoping to catch the wall that led to the stairs. Crying out in fear, I almost hit my head on the stone wall but felt relieved to have made it. A small victory quickly led to the gift of pain from my insides that released its fury. I cried out as I could feel the warmth of blood beginning to drip down the side of my leg. No, I thought, not now. A whimper escaped my lips as I sat on my knees with the wall as support. There was still time if I could only make it to the street.

With each labored breath, I gathered my strength to continue on. The window for meeting Jesus of Nazareth was growing short, shorter than the breaths that I took. It felt as if my efforts were in vain trying to reach the doorway to my house before it was too late. Once the crowd passed by, the chance to meet him would become only a fleeting memory of a missed opportunity. I voiced a silent prayer to God to give me the strength to carry on. As I reached the door to my house to look through, I breathed a sigh of relief when I could see that the crowd had come much closer, but not yet passed me by. I walked a few steps towards the crowd, but my strength failed me, and I fell to my knees. Even if I had to approach Jesus as a beggar, it would not stop me. I began to crawl my way towards the outside of the crowd.

Each time that I could catch a glance of Jesus through the crowd, I could see that his face was full of compassion, but stricken with weariness as a soldier in the heat of battle. There were no signs of anger as the crowds pressed around him. Love for the broken and hurting could be seen through his eyes, mirroring the actions he took for others. His caring for those around him was like a father to his children. His voice softened my soul and quickened my heart. His words sunk deep to the core of my being like a rock falling to the bottom of the sea as they spoke of truth and compassion.

I did not notice until the brick in my heart hit the bottom of the ocean floor, breaking me into tears.

I crumbled in hurt and pain. Nowhere to turn, no place to go. Would a Rabbi such as he ever care enough to heal me? Would he look at a lost soul with those same eyes of compassion? Just maybe, if I could only touch the edge of his cloak then I could feel some comfort in my agony. If I could only taste a drop of the living water, to take the smallest portion I could, then maybe it would be enough for me. I didn't need much; I didn't ask for much. He would not know that I am in

pain or alive. What could I give to a man such as him? He came for others, but not possibly for me.

I just wanted to reach and touch His cloak. It was all I hoped for.

If I could just crawl on my hands and knees. To approach with my face scraping the ground that others walked on. I have nothing to be proud of, nothing to keep me from being judged. The crowd parted as it approached me, flowing around me as if they represented the Red Sea itself. All I had to do was get close enough to Jesus, relying on hope and my small sliver of faith. I had to know if he was real, that His power could heal a broken soul such as I.

I reached out, blinded by the crowd, my desperation for healing the only thing that kept me focused. My fingers grazed the cloak, touching the edges of the thick cloth. I felt and sensed the power of life flow through my fingers like the rushing force of a mighty river.

A voice, filled with compassion and love, in that very moment said, "Your faith has healed you. Go in peace."

I dared not look up as his hand and warmth fell upon my head. Was this the Messiah that truly came to serve and heal those who were lost, like me? Tears filled my eyes as I lay prostrate with my head to the ground, daring not to look up or move as the crowd continued on its way, following Jesus as he moved like someone on a mission.

As the noise quieted around me, the realization began to set it. Faith had healed me and the pain was gone. Jesus brought me life anew that no others were able to do. Thankfulness and praise to God filled my heart where only pain had previously made its home. My old life was no more and a new life had just begun.

FORGIVENESS IN REPENTANCE

In the darkness I tried to hide
Keeping my sin pushed to the side
I had no one that I could trust
Not a soul, not even if I must

Hiding in my sin I could not sleep
My heart pounded as if it tried to leap
The transgressions that I often committed
Were ones that I wished could be omitted

Your hand on me was too heavy to bare
I could not forget or turn away without a care
Day after day I struggled and tried to fight
You wouldn't let go, even deep into the night

You humbled me to the point of defeat
I could no longer hide or live in deceit
To you I confessed my sin and shame
That which before I was too afraid to name

You forgave my sin and rescued me with your hand
You took away the pain and allowed me to stand
You instructed and led me in the path I should go
Loving me as the Father that I have come to know

THE HOUSE (PART 2) – THE LIVING ROOM

I barely used my kitchen. It felt like a waste of time and space to sit there and eat by myself. As soon as my TV dinner was nuked in the microwave after a long day of work, I would walk into my living room and fall onto my couch. With my dinner in hand and a good movie on TV, I would quickly forget about work and everything else that had happened during the day. It was a routine, a tradition, to spend the entire evening in the living room. Only on the weekends would I find time to do the necessary chores or go out of the house. My living room was the only good part of my life before Jesus, so of course it would still be there after I was saved.

Now that I had Jesus as a roommate, I thought it would be a good way for the both of us to connect and relax together in the living room. There was a whole set of movies and video games that I had to show him, hoping he would find enjoyment in the same entertainment that I did. We would laugh at the most hilarious parts of movies and become expert marksmen in my favorite online video games.

Though, how it all turned out was not what I originally envisioned. It became very difficult to convince Jesus to even enter the living room. He had a strong dislike for my kind of entertainment and all the fun that came with it. At first the arguments with Jesus revolved around how my time wasn't being used wisely. This made me very upset. How could he have the audacity to say that I'm wasting my time? What else was I supposed to do in the evenings after work? It was a time to unwind and relax from a long day. Without my TV, there would be nothing to help me work out the stress that built up from work. I needed an outlet and this was it.

Granted, Jesus didn't say I had to give it all up. That was just an exaggeration to his comments about time. He just did not see a use of it and how it negatively affected my life and thoughts. He kept going on about how we have to see the world through His eyes and not from what we watch on TV. I had my reservations, mostly because I didn't know what he meant about looking at the world through his eyes. Jesus did bring other suggestions to replace this time in the evening like calling friends, talking to my neighbors, reading the Bible, or getting more involved in a church community, but these ideas were not something I wanted to do or found interesting. The evenings were my time, and I didn't want this time to end or to be replaced with something that would require me to build relationships with others. Yes, it sounded selfish, but who wouldn't think the same?

I was irritated and upset that Jesus would not join me in the evenings or that he didn't approve of it. But, it didn't stop me from spending money for the new video game I wanted that next day and using all my free time to play through it. It felt good to beat the game and it pleased me much. If only Jesus could see the fun that this brought, then he wouldn't be so against it. Yes, we barely saw each other that week, but that wasn't my fault. I accomplished what I set out to do, which was to beat the new game.

Yet, something didn't sit right with me. I realized a few days later that the feeling of beating the game had gone and I was craving something new. The game lost its value. I remember having this emptiness before I met Jesus, but now, for some reason, it was more…noticeable? Yes, that's it. It was as if I knew that this was not what I was meant to be doing with my life. I grew irritated once again with these thoughts in my head. I knew Jesus had put them there on purpose and it gave me mixed emotions. Was he intruding too far or simply trying to help me? It was as if my flesh was fighting against my spirit for control.

The next day I decided to confront Jesus about this. I wanted to know why these feelings were affecting me. Was playing a video game so bad for me?

When I approached him that day, he looked at me with concern in his eyes before he spoke. "Many have walked astray due to the cares of this world and the deceitfulness of worldly pleasures. The seeds are sown amongst thorns and proven to be unfruitful. I will not let that happen to you."

His words were firm and on point, and it gave me a lot to think about that evening. There was this warm fuzzy feeling that let me know I was loved, but did I trust him? I had never thought about what Jesus was trying to say before now, but as I lay down to sleep that night, it hit me like a ton of bricks. I was truly wasting my life away. Years had gone by and what did I have to show for it? Would anyone care about the video games I played or the accomplishments that came from them? Is it something that I want written in my obituary or that people remember about me? There was more to life than this and Jesus was right; I would have no spiritual fruit to show for it. These thoughts circled inside my head as I lay on the pillow, unable to fall asleep.

The following morning, I did my best to get ready for work but having little sleep, it was difficult to make it through the work day. Tiredness made everything go by much slower than usual and all I wanted to do was go home, relax, and watch a movie in the living room.

It took me only a few minutes to get comfortable, warm up food, and lay down on the couch. I put on one of my favorite movies to help me unwind. I figured Jesus wouldn't join me for it, so I didn't bother to ask him to join or ask for his thoughts on what I wanted to watch. The movie was the only thing on my mind at that point in time. I already made up my mind to spend less time in the living room playing video games, but for days like this, I needed the downtime.

But then something happened. Jesus came in to the living room and sat next to me. I found it odd, but didn't question it. He must have his reasons, and sure enough, they soon became clear. As the movie was playing, Jesus began to make continuous commentary about the scenes that I was watching. He made comments about violence and how it affected my brain. Then the unnecessary gore that prevailed on the images on the screen. This followed by the unwholesome language that the characters used throughout almost every scene. Jesus wanted to let me know that this language would be remembered and used by me in conversations with others. I initially tried to refute him, but it was difficult when I found it to be true.

The worst part was when the sex scene showed up in the movie. I never felt bothered by it, but Jesus definitely did. He described it as pornographic, cruel, and evil. It didn't feel like it to me, but then he kept talking about how it objectified women to entice men and made them less than they were. It was not how God had created women to be, which were made in God's image. God created men and women to be part of a healthy marriage, not something used for pleasure or money outside of it. This was evil in Jesus' eyes. The sadness of how Jesus described it made me finally turn off the movie. I couldn't enjoy it any longer after everything that I had now become aware of.

As I sat there, Jesus transitioned me away from the subject of the movie by asking me about my friend Matthew. "How is he doing?" Jesus said. I shrugged as if it didn't matter. We only talked occasionally on the weekends when we went out to a bar. Though, Jesus kept persisting, asking me to call him and ask.

Eventually, I gave in and called Matthew. It didn't take long to figure out that he wasn't in a good place at all. We talked for an hour and made plans to hang out during the weekend. Before Matthew hung up, he told me, "Thank you for calling. I was in a very bad place tonight and needed someone to talk to." I was surprised and had no idea that Matthew was in such a bad place. Normally, the idea to call someone would not have crossed my mind because of the time I spent playing video games and watching TV throughout the evening.

I looked over at Jesus after I hung up and said, "How did you know?" He only smiled and said that he had tried to tell me to call him for the past couple weeks, but I had been too engrossed in my new video game to listen. I sighed, and realized now that building relationships couldn't be done when using the TV. No matter how I felt about my movie at that time, the opportunity to talk to my friend and help him felt much more rewarding.

As time went by, and with the help of Jesus, my living room soon changed. Yes, the TV remained, but most of the movies were thrown out and I kept only a few of the video games that wouldn't take up a lot of time if I put it in. Then I bought a few new pieces of furniture to make the living room into a place where people could come over and sit. It was just the beginning, but I knew that this change would be for the better. Maybe someday it would be used as a place to socialize with friends or host a church group. The thoughts of bringing others over had only just begun to form in my mind. With Jesus' help, any change was possible.

Now it was just a matter of discipline to keep myself focused and occupied, and to listen to Jesus for any person whom he wanted me to reach out to. Yes, things would be different, but for some reason, the burden of needing entertainment in my life had lifted. It didn't feel as important as it used to. The difference was stark and would take time to get used to, but I could live with it.

TAKING OUT THE TRASH

The worst part was not realizing the conditions that I had been living in. A foul odor enveloped the room, and I couldn't believe that it had never affected me in such a way before. How could I even step back into my room without wanting to throw up? Was there anything clean in my bedroom that was worth keeping? A brief glance around, and it all looked to be trash; garbage that was worthless and not meant to be kept. The only clean things were the clothes I had on upon my return. It would take days to find anything worth keeping, months to put in order, and years to organize.

No, I thought to myself, everything had to go! I knew it to be true, but that was the hardest part. I had no idea where to begin. All the baggage and pain from my old self lay in heaps over the floor, creating an unwholesome stench. The moment of clarity that had come while I was gone did not bring a cleansing of the consequences for my actions in my prior life, but had helped me to see clearly for the first time.

I brought the cleaning supplies (which didn't look to be enough), and I knew what had to be done; it just seemed overwhelming. How did I not know or care about the actions I took in life and what it would bring? Society had told me that I was free from the consequences of my actions, free to live how I wanted, and free to be selfish. Now it was too late to change what I had done or remove the outcome. I had to deal with the past in the present so I could move into the future, and this required me to begin by cleaning up my mess.

Yet, it was a slow process, slower than I wished for. The problem wasn't the surface of the room, but the cupboards, dresser drawers, under and behind the bed, in the mattress, and all the nooks and crannies that any dirty bedroom could possibly hold. These problem areas, these dirty parts of my room made cleaning

the surface areas seem like a walk in the park. The room may look in order after a few months, but the cleaning would only become tougher as time went on. I'm sure that there would always be something missed that I could find later. The cleaning supplies would need a proper and permanent spot next within my closet.

These missed areas of my room will show up when I least wanted to deal with cleaning it. It would be revealed by its smelly odor and affect my life with its slime and guck. No matter what the problem would be, now it was less someone else's fault, but rather something that I wished to fix. It was harder this way, but I found that it helped mend relationships with family or friends who used to be blamed as the cause for all my problems. This was the worst part.

When I was given a new life through Jesus' forgiveness, I thought that all my mistakes and failures were removed and wiped clean. In essence, they were, but not the consequences that my past sins had caused, nor the habits or issues that I failed to realize were still part of my life. I had to clean these things out of my room one-by-one and some hidden ones I didn't know were there to be found. These sinful habits hid themselves in the nooks and crannies, closets, and under the bed. Until it could be found and exposed by the light, I had to have the courage to confront them.

I did not want to clean up the mess of my room, especially when I knew of the pain and hurt this mess had caused others. I wanted to have a blank slate wiped clean, a perfect life, and to have all my old baggage removed once and for all. Yet, it was not so and this could never be the case. My consequences and my old habits had to die, but I had to work to throw them out by cleaning out the trash from my room. It will take time, it will be difficult, but God had given me the cleaning supplies I needed. Now all I had to do was to begin by removing the odor that lingered and to be humble, ready to tackle any area of my room that was next on the list or hid itself from sight. I knew God expected me to have a holy room because He had come to live with me and I would be his forever.

THE FOREST

The trees were sparse and far between as I approached the edge of the forest. It was calm and peaceful with the sun shining through the tree tops and giving off plenty of light. Its appearance showed no signs of deceit and it was inviting me into its presence. Compared to the desert landscape that had only bushes, sand, and rocks, the forest provided both relief and comfort. Food was easy to come by and a small creek gave me fresh water that never dried up. Life was sweet and carefree.

Finding my way out would have been easy as the desert remained in sight and not far away. But I saw no need in a return to my life in the desert after finding the forest to the east. This sanctuary was much deserved and well earned. As the days turned into weeks, the hardships remembered from the desert life began to dissipate and I found myself growing more relaxed and happier.

The weeks turned into months, and I began to prefer the trees over the sunlight and moved further into the forest's nurturing embrace. The desert disappeared and the sun's light found less places to shine through, but it never bothered me. The pull of the forest had no cause for alarm and its invitation to continue on promised me further peace and happiness. The perception of time faded as the forest became more a part of my life than it had been before.

As the days went on, the cover of the trees blotted out the sun and it became as a permanent roof over my head. It promised me more protection than what the sun could have given, and I trusted it and welcomed the light from the luminous insects around and the warmth from the trees. I had wandered in the thick of the forest for months, unable to see the sun beyond the cover of the trees and unable to track the direction or destination that I was heading. Turning back meant knowing how to get out, but at this point I was unsure if this was even possible, or even if I wanted to. The path behind me was covered up and the only way I could go was the trail in front of me. I had slowly lost the freedom that the desert had given me. Yet, something kept pulling me further into the darkness where the days started to become darker and colder. I did not have the power to turn aside from its calling or stay in the comfort of the areas that were warmer and more relaxed. It wooed me and called my name softly, putting me into a trance as if it was a siren on a small island in the sea, hypnotizing me into its dark and deadly embrace.

The whispering voice carried itself through the movement of the trees and the insects which made their home in the ground and bushes surrounding me. The calling of my name had been subtle at first, but the further I walked, the stronger it became. I knew that I did not have the will power to pull away anymore, and I was stuck, chained to the forest which I had initially only considered as a reprieve from the harsh desert climate. It never occurred to me that I would ever venture into its inner depths and darkness. The tranquility and comfort of the trees and their shade had pulled me away from the desert land and the strength of the sun. I hadn't seen the forest for what it was until its roots and branches were fully wrapped around my legs. I was deeper into darkness than I had ever wished to be without any ability or desire to pull myself out.

A sudden sadness overtook me as I sat on a broken tree stump in the darkness of the forest. The path forward only led to death and I knew that, I knew it, but I could not change my direction. I was chained within the forest and its dark and haunting interior. It deprived me of all things and it cried out for my soul, reaching for it, pulling it from me. How could I fight it? I was lost and alone with my thoughts, focused on this meaninglessness pursuit. I knew it led to death, but how could I turn around? No light could shine through, no guide for turning back, and all hope was lost. I walked the line between death and life, and I slipped. Now…well, now all I could live with was regret.

My energy and strength began to seep from my body as I sat. The forest required me to keep moving so time couldn't be spent in regret or to think about my predicament. I was not far from the end of the path set before me, and I saw the signs all around. The bones of others who had come before me lay scattered around the forest floor. Many had died within its deadly embrace without any signs of struggle or panic. The forest's dark interior was not full of life as it promised

me, but full of death. It was a graveyard for the sins of those who had lived their lives stuck in the passions of the flesh.

And here I am, finding a brief moment to reflect and envisioning myself added to the bones around. There is no other path set out before me, no other hope that I could find except that one ray of light that somehow never stopped finding its way through the forest's thick canopy. Was it a path to help me get out? Could there be a chance for a savior to guide me back to the desert land with a bright sun to guide me? Maybe all I needed was a savior to give me strength and courage.

ADRIFT

It was supposed to be a simple voyage, an overnight cruise, a relaxing exercise. Who knew that rowing a boat would end up being so complicated? The directions at the start were quite simple, or so I was told by the dockmaster. I had all I needed. Food for the trip, enough water to last me for weeks, a compass, a map of the stars for direction, and a nice round hat to protect me from the beating sun.

If there had been any other way to get to the other side, I would've taken it in a heartbeat. Blast me off in a catapult for all I cared, as long as the other side had a nice landing pad it would be all right. The easy way out is always the best. Who wants to work hard when there's a better way? Not I.

The directions looked easy enough that a simpleton such as I would have no problem to navigate. At least that's how they pitched it to me. Once I knew my purpose in life, which was to get to the other side, then it was all about finding the means to get there. If it was a rowboat, then so be it. I was supremely confident that it would all work out. I could never have imagined rowing would be so difficult!

I didn't lose focus at first. As long as I was able to see the land behind me, there was always a chance to turn around, which I thought about doing so many times. And maybe that was part of the reason behind my current predicament. You can only turn the boat around so many times before dizziness sets in and any sense of direction is lost.

Then came those nasty clouds. I called them nasty, not because of the rain that came, but because they obscured by vision of the stars at night. It was hard to keep track of my direction without the north star pointing the way. Hard mode was already trying to use the map without any help or guidance, and then the heavens thought that "God mode" was more suitable because only God could navigate these skies.

But, I do have to admit my own faults on this whole mess. As with most people, my left arm is stronger than the right, so naturally this caused me to row the boat in a westerly direction. Well, at first it was a westerly direction, but it may have turned into a circular one. Correcting this after finding the fault didn't solve the problem I created. And that's on top of all the indecision I had when I couldn't make up my mind about turning back around. Now, I'm stuck asking myself several questions.

Where was I?

Oh yes, I am lost. Truly lost. I probably should have noticed this early on, but it took me a few days without land in sight to admit this to myself. And yes, stubbornness kept me from admitting this much earlier. Of course, the blame should mostly lie with those nasty clouds and not because of anything I did. So here I am, without proper guidance and direction, adrift in the middle of the ocean and no way to know where I was or how to correct my course.

How did I get here?

I thought I was ready for this journey, preparing everything I could think of before setting out. Nothing had been lacking and checking the list thrice over helped calm my worries and anxieties. Even the dockmaster assumed I was overthinking everything. I mean, who is he to assume I wouldn't come prepared? The audacity! I am still upset at him questioning my preparedness even with the help he gave. Well, whatever help he did give me was obviously not enough. Got me lost is what it did. That's two strikes against him. He probably committed a third one that I'm yet aware of.

When am I going to take action and do something?

All this reminiscing of past mistakes only prolongs the inevitable. Sitting in a boat out in the ocean can do this to you. Too much idle time to think and not enough time to solve the current predicament. It must be because thinking of a solution requires me to stop ignoring where I am. It's just easier to solve the problem of how I got here rather than how I am to get out of this spot. I had a whole list of excuses and one long essay to explain away my faults. If there was just one person with me to talk to rather than my own thoughts, it would have been extremely helpful and possibly even bearable.

What should I do?

The problem that surrounded me was simple. And yes, the problem was the ocean itself. How to remove this was probably not going to work. Evaporation only works so fast. I got everything I needed but not the experience to know how to proceed. There was a map of the stars, the paddles, and even a simple compass to guide me. Yet, taking a course in navigation is not the same as when you try it out for the first time. Too many unaccounted variables and unexpected scenarios. For example, those nasty clouds that keep showing up in the sky. But, at some point I had to make a commitment on the next step.

Who am I?

I must go back in the past again. Why did I set out on this journey to begin with? I barely remember it all, but it was something with having figured out my purpose in life. Purpose set me on this journey and purpose gave me the will to do it. I had forgotten. For some reason, in the middle of preparing for my journey, I lost the focus of why I was leaving and where my destination was. Purpose. Ahh yes, the purpose came about because I figured out who I finally am. When I found out how God loved me and that I was created in His image, then I knew that my journey would lead to this far distant island. Yes, I remember it all now. The purpose was what was supposed to guide me, not my tools. Forgetting my purpose created indecision and a loss of direction. But how can I fix it now?

I took a deep breath and steadied myself. Part of what I knew had to be done was to focus again on my purpose. A few moments passed by and I opened my eyes. Immediate disappointment ensued because I was not docked on the opposite side! Ugh! This miracle must've been too much to ask for. Then I looked up and saw it. Was this mast here all along? A small mast with a sail sat on the bottom of the boat. I hurriedly worked to get the sail unraveled. Now, it was all about positioning and wind.

To my astonishment, the wind started to pick up, and I laughed to myself. At least this miracle was possible! Finally, something good! Now if those nasty clouds would not show up again, I could finally direct this boat to where I have to go. Just have to keep steady and remember my purpose to reach the destination set before me.

THE PUNCHING BAG

The punches that came at me felt slow and telegraphed. I was ready for them and able how to deflect or block each and every combination. There was an assurance in my movements as my feet held firm on the solid floor below. No punch, no jab, nothing surprised me; I held my ground and could not be pushed into the ropes. I was ready to step into this fight after prior failures and setbacks, and felt strong enough to finally endure it.

As the fight grew fiercer, I could see the sweat rolling down my body like dew flowing down a leaf in the early morning sunrise. Yet, there was no fear nor any attack that could overwhelm me. Jesus taught me to stand firm, and stand I did. I danced and moved around the ring, blocking the punches from my foe who tried to knock me into the ropes. Some made their way through, but they felt light, and I was able to shake it off. It took concentration and effort, but ever since I had learned where my strength truly lies, confidence quickly built within me. Nothing could deter me, and I had the courage to stand toe-to-toe with the evil one for as long as it took. I began to throw some counterpunches with the hope that he would flee from the ring and admit defeat.

Yet, something felt off, the longer the fight went on my confidence in him leaving began to faulter. For some reason my ability to stand strong did not have the desired effect any longer. A smile crept onto my enemy's face as he stood fighting in what looked like a losing battle. Anger crept in as I wanted to wipe that grin off his ugly face. It pushed me to fight him with more effort and force, and as he backed towards the ropes, my confidence grew once again. I began to feel pride in my prowess to push the attack and overpower the enemy that stood before me. I had been no match with him some time ago, but now my skills and talent proved to be too much for him. It was a gift of mine to fight - a skill that was honed and sharpened - and fight I did.

I had my enemy almost to the ropes when my footing began to slip. I tried to step forward, but instead found myself struggling to remain balanced. My feet felt like they were standing on ice. Gritting my teeth, I let out a growl and pushed forward nonetheless. It was then that my advantage was lost. The counterpunches came and nearly knocked me to the ground. I did my best to block against the blows, but it was too much to handle on my own. I started to lose ground slowly, unable to handle the onslaught that had come at me in full force.

Tiredness and fatigue began to set in as blocking the enemy's assault on my body seeped all the energy from my muscles. The confidence in my own abilities quickly faded. In my pride, I had pushed the attack and gone astray from the plan that was originally given by my trainer. With my mind focused on myself and pride setting in, it was all that the enemy needed to take the advantage. He knew my weakness and had smiled during the fight knowing that my pride would lead to a change in strategy. The enemy's punches started to pour on my body. Hit after hit jabbed into my very soul. I started to falter and my footing slipped as I staggered into the ropes behind me.

I was no longer the stronger boxer; I was the punching bag of an enemy who had taken control. No retaliation could come from my end, no hits could I send back. This time the punches felt hard and faster than ever before. I tried to bring my arms up over my head, hoping to block the hits from landing on my face. It did not help, as I felt my lower body getting punched and breaking me apart slowly one hit at a time. I knew, if this continued, the battle would be lost and the enemy would have its victory.

How was I going to turn this around?

I felt like giving up in that moment, to let the punches end my life. I was no more than a punching bag to the enemy and unable mount any comeback. How could I stand up to fight again? How had I stood stall and firm in the first place? I needed to remember, to understand what the key was that I had missed along the way.

Pride.

Yes, pride had ruined it for me. I thought that I could do this fight on my own without God's help. There was no humility left. I had shifted my reliance on God to myself. There was this thought that my own strength could overpower the enemy and make him flee from me. But this was conceited. Nothing I could do on my own would be enough. I knew this deep inside and it was how this fight had turned against me. The slow jabs and light punches from my enemy were an outcome of God's power and not my own. As soon as I had turned from God's help, the enemy knew it was the time to strike.

I was at the end of myself and could not go on. I needed God's power to regain my footing and keep fighting. A part of me had to change and it was the pride which had built up within my soul. I asked God with all the strength I had left to remove the sin and to once again help me win the fight. It wasn't long before my energy and strength returned and the ground below my feet became solid once again. It was a power that came from above and nothing from my own being.

The enemy hesitated to strike and his smile quickly failed as if realizing that his final assault had not been successful. As he tried to hit me with his best combinations, I found myself seeing his jabs easily once again, and quickly countered. I knew that this time I had to stick to the gameplan and not rely on myself to win the fight.

God was by my side, like the trainer in the corner between rounds, giving me the strength to stand up and re-enter the ring. He helped me see my weaknesses and failures and trained me to stand tall with courage and strength that flowed out through him. By trusting in his plan, I could make the enemy flee and surrender. Nothing in this fight was easy, but I would never again forget where my strength came from. I would never again do this fight alone.

I thanked God for staying with me as the trainer by my side. Only he could provide for me, I knew. I could take the punches again, but this time with renewed focus, renewed faith, and renewed hope.

FORSAKEN AND FORGOTTEN

Life seems unfair and it can change so suddenly. The car accident wasn't my fault as I only happened to be at the wrong place at the wrong time. The drunk driver had walked away almost unscathed while I ended up paralyzed from the waist down. I would live the rest of my life in a wheel chair and the hopes and dreams that had stood in front of me now lay empty and shattered. There was nothing left for me; I was both forsaken and forgotten by all, a lonely soul who would forever need help to survive.

Today was my release date from the hospital, but I was far from ready, far from accepting the reality that lay before me. The wheel chair lay ominously by my side, ready for me sit down and move around. Yet, staying in my hospital bed meant that there would still be a chance for healing and a miracle. Family and friends had prayed over me, but there was no answer, no favorable outcome to my situation. I was truly forgotten by God.

My body ached, pleading its case within my mind. It craved to be used as it grew weak from the motionless state that it found itself in. The muscles cried out in a desperate measure to reason with my thoughts, but its voice landed on deaf ears. The severed spine had cut all communication and feeling. Atrophy was beginning its work and nothing could stop it. The muscles built to move with freedom would now look skinny and sickly.

There would be no length of waiting, no healing to cure my condition.

I knew not the difficulties that lay before me or the physical needs that were to come. Only my mental fortitude kept me from falling into complete despair. Yes, I still had my mind, but it was a two-edged sword. It would not let me forget the accident that crippled me, but it also gave me reasons to carry on and make the best of my situation, showing me that there was still hope. Yet, who could uplift

HOSPITAL

my downtrodden soul? It only proved that my spiritual needs outweighed that which hindered my physical movements.

An answer.

Yes, that is what I wanted to hear.

God had been silent for too long; no healing, no hope, no answer. Did He even try to stop the drunk driver from swerving when he did? There was no moment of clarity from up above and I needed it more than ever before. The anger inside of me began to grow steadily like a kettle coming to a slow boil. What is taking God so long? Why were some people healed and others left crippled? Life was far from fair and I had gotten the short end of the stick.

No sound from God penetrated the room that I found myself in. I could hear the sound of my own breathing, the beeping of the machines, and the noise from the patients next to me, but nothing from God Himself.

Yes, the silence. Did He even know that I existed? Could God not answer or give me the healing that I so greatly needed? Was I not important to Him anymore?

I was forsaken and forgotten.

What meaning is there to life if God would not bless me in the time of my utmost need? I didn't want to move or leave the hospital bed. No, moving was out of the question and not because of my paralysis. My body will grow stale from lying here, but that was already bound to happen to my legs anyway. If I moved now, it would be without any purpose or meaning to my life. I needed an answer and only God could provide it.

An answer.

Yes, that is what I wanted to hear.

Would the answer come? That was my greatest prayer. Life paralyzed me and kept me from doing what I wanted to do. I needed to act but acting required faith that God will move in my life. And lying in bed required God to move and not I. Stubbornness made me who I was, and if I only kept praying, then my healing would come or the true purpose for my life.

An answer.

Yes, that is what I wanted to hear.

But deep down I knew it was my pain from losing out.

The door opened and the nurse stepped in. The light shined brightly as it penetrated the darkness that had engulfed the room. It brought comfort and peace that removed the darkened thoughts from my mind. There would be no going back, no turning around or sleeping through the sadness when I exited the room. I had to go on and live my life as best as I could. It would not be easy, nothing like this ever was, but maybe God would remember me and provide the answer that I so desperately asked for.

THE BANQUET

But when you give a feast, invite the poor, the crippled, the lame,
the blind, and you will be blessed, because they cannot repay
you. For you will be repaid at the resurrection of the just.
-Luke 14:13-14

The footsteps echoed throughout the dining hall as I paced back and forth. It was the night before the big banquet, and everything was prepared. The servants had gone home for the evening and it was only my presence that filled the hall. It is my first big party, the celebration of my success and accomplishments which had set me apart from my peers. I became so rich that few could compete, even to build a mansion such as this.

Though, I never cared much for the money. My concern was losing those friendships from before I gained my fortune and fame. If I couldn't celebrate everything with them, then who? What was this fame without friends and what is fortune when you have nobody to share it with?

It all began falling apart a couple days ago. My butler brought the first few messages from my invited guest list. Each response took a piece of my joy away. All the friends whom I invited were providing reasons to be excused from my banquet. Some had urgent matters to attend out of town, others had double booked events and did not consider mine as the priority, and still more found any and every reason to decline the invitation.

Who would come in the end? The question bothered me as a paced the great banquet hall. I was the one who had always been there for them and who came when a crisis happened. No matter what, my presence and support was provided to others. But what about me? When my time came, who would be there but myself? Are all others so selfish with their time as to only go to events that benefited them?

Did money bother others so much? If so, then I would not have wished this fame on anyone. It had become like a curse. No happiness and joy came with money, only loneliness and anguish. Was it simply envy and jealousy that justified breaking friendships? I thought maybe my character and love for others would shine through despite the fortune I made, but I was mistaken. People are who they are and it is hard to live with this when reality sets in. The tables with their fine cutlery and immaculate design stood empty in the moonlit night and they would remain so tomorrow for the banquet. Nothing would be touched. It would remain clean as it came in and would remain clean as it would be removed. The meal for a lifetime would go to waste and all the gifts thrown out. Everything set out I would've given with no strings attached and nothing required in return. It was all for my guests and friends, to all who would come, to them I would treasure and adore. It was meant to be a banquet for the ages, a time for joy and celebration.

Yet, the vision of what would be only made it as far as what was in my dreams. Reality is harsh and unreliable. Innocence is replaced with pain when sin cannot be ignored and one's heart is broken.

I was at an impasse. No where to go, no shame too great. An empty banquet, decorated for all, but for none to see. Food for all, but none would be eaten. Music for all to hear and dance to, but none would experience.

Pain turned to sorrow, and my sorrow turned to anger. If they did not want my joy, then they would not get it. I would cut them off, throw them away and never speak with them again. I wanted to punish them for their selfish desires. Maybe I would be alone, but at least no one would be able to hurt me again. There would be no need to feel embarrassed and sad at the time when happiness should fill the air.

The windows to the banquet hall were open to cool the room and circulate fresh air. As the wind blew the light curtains, it brought with it playful noises that made me look and see where it came from. As I peered out the window, I could make out the shadows of two kids playing in the garden. Their curiosity and playfulness reminded me of my youth as their innocence and imagination carried them to places that others wouldn't dare to venture. They must've scaled the wall and found out what was on the other side.

Something in me wanted to meet these two kids. I called for them and beckoned them over. At first, I could only hear the calm of the night as the playful voices were silenced by my call. They may have been scared or worried that they were in trouble, and I knew that this would seem odd to them. How would they know that I meant no harm?

I called again and tried to reassure them that everything was okay. A few more minutes passed, and I thought my opportunity was gone, but soon I heard some movement behind one of the bushes and I could see that their curiosity got the best of them. I called once more, and they looked around to make sure it was only me and not anyone else in the garden as they slowly made their way over to the window. The closer they got, I could see that they were not the kids of any of the neighbors, but must've come from across the river and the poverty-stricken neighborhood that made its home there.

As they got close enough to where they could see me, I gave them a warm smile and let them know that they had done no harm to my garden.

"How did you get in?" I asked, being more curious than accusatory in my tone.

The taller kid with scuffled short hair replied by pointing at a corner of the brick wall where a tree had grown close and a thick branch dipped over and down. I had never thought about this as a reason to get into my garden, and chuckled some. It was perfectly placed to get out as well. The kids saw my reaction and their body language showed that they could trust me more than at first. I wanted to continue the conversation and asked them what they were doing there.

The same kid spoke for the first time, "we heard you would have a big banquet and wanted to see for ourselves."

It made sense, I thought to myself. Many of the servants who worked for me came from the neighborhood across the river. They must've been excited for the event just as much as me. I gestured them to come close to the window and look in at the empty banquet hall. Their eyes were filled with amazement at all the fine cutlery and tables that was perfectly placed throughout.

Before I could say something more, the shorter kid spoke. "Mister," he said, "how many will be at your party? Can we come? We will be in the back with our aunts in the kitchen and…" The taller kid and who must've been the older quickly hit the other kid in the arm to quiet his curiosity and unfiltered questions.

I tried to formulate my response to an unexpected question.

Hearing my lack of a quick reply, the taller kid asked in what he deemed a better way. "Mister, we wanted to know if there would be any work for us in the back so we could see the banquet?"

I could tell that they wanted to experience something that they had never seen before in their lives. They were still not fully understanding of the social order of things and only wanted to partake in something that seemed so wonderful and extraordinary. Their innocence broke me and no longer could I feel the anger from past friends, but only the compassion for those who seemed so innocent and carefree. They had what I missed, and it was the love of friends and family. I said that they were more than welcome to not only come, but to have seats at the banquet tomorrow. Their eyes grew so big, and their smiles filled their face from ear-to-ear. They kept repeating "thank you sir," and their joy seemed to overwhelm everything around. They excused themselves to run back home and to tell their friends and family. I knew that they would take the opportunity to tell everyone they knew.

As I left the banquet hall and made my way to the sleeping chambers, I had an idea that seemed crazy at first, but the more I thought about it, the happier I felt. That night I fell asleep with a smile and a newfound joy that I thought was long forgotten.

I woke up earlier than anybody else that day. There was no time to wait, and I had to quickly help everyone get ready in order to carry out the task in short notice. I told my butler to gather everyone around as soon as they arrived, all the maids, the cooks, the doormen, the gardeners, and anyone else I could find and had them congregate in the foyer. Everyone seemed curious to this sudden and unexpected gathering, and no one had any idea what was going on. As they grew in anticipation of what was to be said, I stood a few steps above to speak and began to tell them all my newly thought-out plans.

"Invite everyone!" I told them. "Your family, friends, and neighbors. This banquet is for you all and I want this hall filled with laughter and joy." They looked shocked at first, not understanding what was happening. I understood their reaction, so I did my best to clarify. "Please, invite everyone you know for tonight. Everyone who was supposed to come have canceled and there is no reason to let all this go to waste." I implored them, "please, please, go and invite everyone for tonight. Go now, go fast."

There were some murmurs at first and objections. "Who will get everything ready?" and "who will serve?" I told them, "Don't worry! Figure out who goes and stays; who serves and eats. We will work together to prepare and serve each other so that everyone can enjoy!"

At first, all the servants were hesitant to leave, but as a few began to depart out the door, the flow continued to steadily increase. Soon the house was empty except for a few elderly servants who decided to stay behind for preparations. It would be a glorious time, with a lively atmosphere that would never be seen before. It would be a time to celebrate life with those whose futures were not tied in wealth, but in love and kindness with each other, who found more joy in celebration than in possessions.

I knew this was much better than the original plan. A time to fill the hall of life with people who wanted to be a part of it. It would be a celebration for the ages. A glorious time indeed!

THE HOUSE (PART 3) – THE PRIVATE OFFICE

My days were spent with a new weekly task after having more free time on my hands. I created this complicated spreadsheet to keep track of all my possessions in each room. Not only was I proud of my newly developed skills in excel, but this was also a way to figure out what Jesus was up to, to find anything else that went missing in my house and when. I believed he was trying to be sneaky, hiding it from me and trying to be quiet about it. No matter what he tried to do, it only caused unwanted and unnecessary drama in my life.

He kept irritating me with these additional requests and had a strong inability to follow orders, almost as if he was expecting the opposite. One of the many problems was his constant failure to comply with keeping out of the areas of my house that was off-limits. It bothered me that he felt like knocking on the door to my private office. This is where I took care of my finances and worked. I felt as if he was trying to solicit me on a continual basis for his services. He told me that he had experience in handling finances and could give me a great work-life balance. Hah! I wouldn't trust my own mother with my finances, much less Jesus.

The crazy thing is, he wanted me to give ten percent of my income to him each month. Ten percent! Doesn't he know that I'm in constant need and inundated with bills? I almost felt like this was his intention all along. Come in to my house, befriend me, try to help me be a better person, and then come after me for his commission and support. Feels like every other scam that has been pitched to me in my life. I should've known that this would happen at some point. Nothing is ever free.

Though, since I was benefiting from his help in other areas of my life, I didn't really want to kick him out of my house just yet. It was a simple thing really, keep my money and private office away from his greedy hands and things would be alright. I was practicing forgiveness anyway, so the least I could do was forgive Jesus for demanding a large commission for taking care of my finances. The government was already taking half my money and it never truly followed up on its promises. So, why trust someone else with the rest? Besides, it's not like Jesus would go on strike and stop helping in my house by demanding payment.

Just like anything in life, it never ends the way you hope. One fateful day it all escalated. Jesus walked unannounced into my office, asking to look at my work files and bank statements. Does he not listen to what I say? I knew what he was doing, trying to make demands of me again, then start doing the work only to charge me for it later. The audacity! Finances are not his concern, nor will it ever be. Who even dares to do such a thing? I was mad, angry, incensed that he stepped out of line. That line being the door to my office. My temper flared. "I control this part of my life, and you stay out!" I yelled. "How dare you think that you know better how to run my finances and my life!?" He kept saying that he had to prepare me for what was to come, as if he was a prophet who knew the future. Definitely not believable.

I had to shove him out and lock the door to my office, refusing to believe that he could help me. I knew exactly what I needed to pay, what I wanted to spend money on, and how to portion my income as such. I felt confident that I could control my money and job and had done so up until this point. The rest of that day I sat brooding in my office, making plans for a possible roommate contract with Jesus so that he doesn't cross this line again.

A few weeks later, everything that could go wrong, went wrong. It was unexpected and came completely by surprise. Just like a low budget horror movie, my company had a breach of contract with a business partner and lost their biggest customer. The layoffs came almost simultaneously. The immediate prayers that I would keep my job went unanswered, mostly because I didn't get the chance to ask for prayer prior to losing my job. It came faster than being kicked in the face by a bucking horse; a shove to the curb with a low-end severance pay that gave me very few options.

I knew not what I would do or how to make it from here. This had been the only job since graduating from college and I grew numb thinking that I had no way to pay for my next month's rent. The realization that I may have to ask my parents for money shattered any sort of pride that I had left in my life. I came home in a sad state and walked straight into my office, refusing to acknowledge the presence of Jesus who looked overly concerned.

I spent days, months in my office, trying to figure out what to do with my life as it crashed down around me, with debt accumulating like an avalanche coming down the side of a mountain. There was nothing to stop things from spiraling out of my control, and I could not piece it back together. There needed to be a way out,

a way to provide me financial security once more. I did everything in my power, but the realization crept in that if things weren't changing soon, I would lose my house. It became more difficult with each passing day to see myself digging out from this mess and it made me sick to my stomach. Job applications came up empty and no one seemed to be hiring, or if they were, my job experience did not match or made me overqualified. Anything I tried to do regarding an income kept falling short. I was running out of time and the knowledge of having to live in my parent's basement once again would permanently put an end to my social life as I knew it.

At my lowest point, I heard a knock on my office door. I knew who it was, but at that point I didn't care. I figured, why not let him in? What harm can Jesus do that the world hadn't already done to me? He can charge ten percent of my income at this point I thought. The jokes on him though because there was no income to take from, and all the work would be for free.

I unlocked the door and let Him in…begrudgingly. He immediately began by pushing me out of my seat, having me sit to the side as He went to the desk and began organizing everything to His liking. At first, He started to cut out all these things that had become part of my life. He removed my cable TV subscription, sold my second car, halved my restaurant and drinks budget, and then halved it again! Then Jesus banned me from most of my favorite top brand clothing stores and perfume brands. I felt as if I should be mad, but I was too worn out to care.

As I sat around my house doing nothing, things started to come back into order. I had no idea how much money I was spending on things that I didn't need in my life. He found me a job that I didn't believe existed and applying for it was a piece of cake. It was a similar pay as my prior job, if not a little less, but I was happy to start working once again. Doing nothing is not what people think it is. We are definitely made to work and stay busy.

I ended up loving my new career more than the one I had before, and I cared more about the work than the prior job. For some reason, the time spent on work decreased and the money left over each month seemed to be much more than before. There were fewer additional costs or payments for things I did not need, and I had more money to spend on a weekly basis. And believe it or not, this was after the ten percent that Jesus asked for each month!

This weight of anxiety and stress left my shoulders that I never knew was there. Maybe it was a good thing to let Jesus have control of this room as well. He seemed up to the challenge and it freed up my time to focus on other things. There was a huge debt to pay off from loaning money while out of a job, but with the additional changes, I would get back into shape very soon. The best thing was that I still had my house.

Jesus approached me as I came home from my new job one day and explained why he had entered my office. He knew that I was going to lose my job and wanted to prepare me for it so that I would not go into the high amount of debt which he had foreseen. I did not understand or realize the long-term consequences and only focused on what I thought was important to me at that moment. All he had in mind was to try and protect me from becoming a slave to money and material possessions. If I had known what financial freedom would look like, I wouldn't have been so stubborn to begin with. I finally felt free, free to use my money to help others and free to spend it on things that truly mattered in this world. Well, once I paid off this debt of course.

Jesus seemed to keep growing on me, but the deeper he went into my house, the harder I resisted.

THE IRONY OF SUCCESS

Very few people know how to use their time wisely, but I was one of them and proud of it. It was important to plan a day instead of sitting around chatting or relaxing. Everything revolved around being efficient and making use of each hour you had. It required discipline and perfection. I had spent hours on self-help books and learning how to be successful. If you could sit around, they would say, then you were losing out on an opportunity to make money. It was with this ideology that I began to live my life.

If learning how to make money was the means, then the end result is sitting at the pinnacle of success. It was also something that my church would teach. If you did what was right, then God would bless you with financial wealth. It was a sign of being good in God's eyes. The money, the success, the glory. It was the ultimate goal in life and it was how I shaped my life. Every minute, every spare moment in time, I looked for ways to better myself and get ahead. There was no time to waste on what others would consider as leisure. I saved all I could by living frugally and working hard, only thinking of the goals I had set before me, and invested every penny. It became a mantra of mine to say, "How can I indulge in wasteful spending if the money isn't available?"

I became like a well-oiled machine, able to discipline myself in all aspects of life so I could find the success that was within reach. It was truly a pursuit of happiness and all the obstacles were removed in the name of Jesus. I felt blessed and on top of the world where I soon became a mentor to others who wanted to be like me. I had begun to produce the fruit of my labor and still I could not relax. There was no time to spare.

In the end, I got what was promised. Success, money, and fame. Yet, my time was still spent doing what I had done all my life…work. No breaks, no time to reflect, and no time for what others freely spent their money on. But as I walked down the streets of the city, I could see families with little to nothing looking happy by living in the moment. Why did it affect me so? Wasn't God blessing me with all his financial wealth and success because of my good works? I had what money could buy and could do anything I wished, but I no longer wanted to do the things that were fun in my youth. I had grown old and the pleasure was found by looking at my bank account and the praise that others gave me on a daily basis.

All that I saved my money for, I no longer wanted to do. I had forsaken everything in my pursuit for success. A family; I chose singleness. Vacations; I chose work. Social gatherings; I chose stocks. Sleeping in; I chose exercise. All that made life worth living was sacrificed in the pursuit of success. I made my time about money, and money consumed me. Was this truly what the Bible taught?

I remember my first set of neighbors before I moved to a bigger house. There was a feeling of resentment and jealousy which had consumed me. He had used his life to build relationships and a family, serving the same God but without having been blessed like me. He had tried to teach me what it meant to live, but the ideas presented by him would've taken away all that I was planning to achieve. Instead I had tried to convince him of all the opportunities to build his financial portfolio that he was wasting away each day and that God would bless him like he had for me. He only looked at me with sadness, and a part of me resented him for it, and I did not know why. Was I trying to convince him or myself that this was the perfect life? Why did he not care that his house wasn't as big as mine or that I could have retired early if I wanted to? I did not understand. I could not comprehend. Yet, something about his life felt right.

Joy had consumed him all the days of his life. His love for others was his motivation, and it had nothing to do with money. I was envious of the happy and carefree life he seemed to have. He had what others told me was a waste of time and what I worked hard not to become. I did not see the point of spending time building relationships, serving those in need, and giving away my money. So why am I the who one is jealous and resentful?

He wasn't blessed with success; I was. He took a day of rest; I did not. He lived in comfort; I lived in luxury. He took vacations; I took on a second job. Through all this, I had to figure out why these feelings of anger against him would not go away. I thought that I didn't want what he had, that his life was missing out on all that there was to achieve. Though, as time had passed me by, I slowly began to see how wrong I was. The irony of success had taken a grip on me. I was held hostage and had revolved my life around what I thought would bring me joy.

What will become of my success and money when I pass away from this earth? I realized there was no way to control how someone would use the inheritance that I would give them. No one seemed able to carry on with the perfection that I had worked so hard to achieve. Instead, all my money would be used by someone who may not care about success, but will use it for all the social gatherings and leisure that I had given up. It was truly an irony.

Time. It had gone by so quickly and barely left a mark in eternity. It had allowed me to store up treasures on earth, but nothing was left for heaven. This world had lied to me and the time spent I could not get back. All the self-help books that I read did not come with the most important disclaimer, that it could not provide a true purpose or meaning. It could not see beyond this short life and the pursuit of empty happiness.

JOB'S LAMENT

And he said, "Naked I came from my mother's womb, and naked
shall I return. The Lord gave, and the Lord has taken
away; blessed be the name of the Lord."
-Job 1:21

I have never felt this pain before, this heartache that tears at the very core of my soul. I wish to forget the day that I was birthed and entered this life. It would have been better than the sorrows that have come my way. I do not understand why God let me live knowing how I would be experiencing the pain that life on this earth has brought and doing nothing about it.

May my days be cursed and forgotten and my name removed from this earth. How I wish that this life could be erased and that darkness covered the day of my birth. That there would not have been any shouts of joy or tears of happiness when that day arrived.

Yet, here I am. Alive, but barely. Covered in boils and sores with my wife and friends unable to grant me solace. I should have been forgotten, left for dead, buried in the ground, and placed with the forgotten rulers and kings of old, the rich princes and their treasures, and the wicked people of past generations. It is a place where slaves are freed, where those who seek to escape from the pain of life can finally rest in peace. Oh, how I search, how I seek to be given relief from this great turmoil that has come upon my life.

Why, my heart wonders, is life given to those who experience misery? Is it meant for the men and women who live a bitter existence on this earth? They often look forward to the death that is to come and rejoice in the day it is given like a

man finding a hidden treasure. I do not understand or know why my suffering has become so great and why my daily food is from the pain that I bear so heavily.

In God I will not curse, in God I will keep my faith. This world may have its pain or its heartache, but my trust will still remain. I may wish for my life to have never begun, but as it has been granted to me, in the Lord I will worship. We are born with nothing and leave this earth taking nothing with us. The Lord gives and He takes away. Blessed is the Lord Almighty.

THE CLOUD

On the morning of the third day there were thunders and
lightnings and a thick cloud on the mountain and a very
loud trumpet blast, so that all the people in the camp trembled.
Then Moses brought the people out of the camp to meet God,
and they took their stand at the foot of the mountain.
-Exodus 19:16-17

The mountain rose high above, its peak disappearing in an ominous cloud that covered its top so that no one could see inside its eternal grip. There was a sense of power emanating from the cloud as it encased the peak, warning anyone who dared to venture too close with bolts of lightning that never traveled far from its fearful and fiery clutches. It darkened the entire sky as if it willed the sun to obey its thunderous voice.

A lesser person may have been intimidated by the sight before me, but not I, not now, not this time. I clenched my jaw and stared into the cloud as if its mighty power could not scare me any longer. Focus, not fear, would guide me in the climb up the face of the mountain. There would be no rest until my goal was achieved and only death could stop me now.

My feet moved forward by sheer will and motivation as I began my ascent. The cloud shifted above as if observing my progression for the first time. It was as if it could see through my intentions and daring me to come closer.

Watching.

Waiting.

Wondering.

The might of the cloud pushed heavily on my shoulders. The weight and pressure grew with each additional step.

The stones echoed in anger as they fell from the side of the mountain and to the valley below. The monotonous tone of the rocks cried out in protest, refusing to keep silent. My fingers grew numb as I grabbed for any and all handholds upon the mountain's edge, failing more often than not. My feet worked tirelessly to find solid footing as I slipped and fell on the gravel that covered the mountainside. Even as blood covered my hands and knees, I would not be deterred, my mind was made up, and I had to keep climbing upward.

A feral growl grew from deep within as my determination kept me moving forward. My instincts to survive the climb had all but taken over as I could feel the edges of the cloud hovering above. My body begged for rest, but I would not have it. I could not have it! The end was in site and my answers would be found there. They had to; they must be. There was no other recourse, no other path to take. The climb was all that mattered. There would be no rest in this life until I reached my goal.

I needed to encounter God face-to-face and this is where he would be, residing on the mountain in the clutches of the ominous cloud. I needed an answer for the pain he caused me, for the happy life I was promised if I believed in him. I wanted to yell at the top of my lungs, to scream my pain, my hurt, and my sorrows into his face. I wanted him to know. I wanted…I... wanted.

My pastor had preached that God had plans to prosper me, but I never saw this prosperity. I kept hoping for change if I just had more faith, but it never materialized as I was promised it would. In the end, sorrow became God's gift to me and sorrow never let go of its hold. It always found its way back into my life. No more; I could take it no more. I had cried out for answers, but all I received was silence. This is why I had to meet God where I knew he would reside. Here the answers would come; here God could not be silent. My petition, my request could not be ignored.

My hand grabbed the ledge that brought me to the cloud's fearful center. It was the first firm grip since starting my ascent. My labored breathing came through parched and heavy as I pulled myself onto the ledge. The rasps were a cry for help,

a wish for the climb to end. It did not matter, nothing else concerned me in this life. The wind blew its chilling breath as I worked to stand on the firm ground; lightning striking around me as the cloud protested my presence within its mighty grip.

I cried out to God, "Tell me why my life isn't prosperous like you promised?"!

Only the howling wind could be heard in response as it passed through the thick cloud, causing me to stumble and fall to my knees.

I would not give up as I roared, "Answer me"!

The wind carried the sound of my voice into the clouds. As if on cue, a bolt of lightning hit the rock wall next to me. The strike careened off of the edge and down the side, as if controlled by a mighty hand, and forced me to cover my ears and close my eyes. I could feel the mountain tremble, shaking at its very core, and all I could do was to push myself against the side of the mountain so I wouldn't fall into the darkness below, crippled by the powerful blast. Several minutes past as my ears and eyes slowly returned to normal and the mountain stood still once again. I continued to cover myself for a while longer in a vain attempt for protection, fearing that another lightning strike would come at any second.

When I finally had the courage to look up, I could see the charred rock where the bolt of lightning had struck. It brought the reality of what had happened a few moments ago. Something seemed odd about the spot in the mountainside, so I slowly crawled along the ledge to where the lightning had hit. Etched into the side of the rock was a shining cross. Confusion crossed my face as I tried to understand its meaning. I had come for answers, but would this be all I got?

My mind raced like never before as I tried to tie the meaning to my situation. Had I missed something along my journey that would unlock the reason for my sorrows? Water droplets started to fall on the ground around me and with each drop the meaning began to take shape.

In my selfishness and sorrow, I had believed a lie. This life was not about me or my prosperity, it never was. My tears mixed with those from the cloud. God gave an answer when he did not have to, a reason for life when I did not want one. He saw my sorrow.

The cloud began to grow thicker as it formed a blanket of comfort, wrapping itself around me. I knew, at that point, that God understood my pain. He had sacrificed his very Son to die for me and he knew what sorrow meant.

I preferred this, I knew, to be in God's presence. I did not want to go back down the mountain and face the pain and sorrows that tormented me so. The hurt that this life caused was too great and all I wanted was to find my rest from this short life. This is the peace that I craved and the peace that I would take with me through the rest of my time on earth. I had found my answer.

THE BEACH

The shoreline lay quiet before me. All the playful voices and sounds of the living had left for the day. Yet, there I sat, unable to move, transfixed by the thoughts which whirled inside my head. The grains of sand sifted between each finger as I moved my hand across its surface. I could feel the heat give way to the coolness that lay below as I dug deeper into the earth. The sand flowed around my skin, its cooling tendrils moving up my hand as if possessing a life of its own, wanting to remove the warmth that the sun had so freely given.

The warmth would soon dissipate, as it always does, flowing in a symbiotic dance with the earth's rotation around the sun. Just like life itself, it ebbs and flows, always with a beginning and always with an end. Time will forget the very clues of my existence, just like the sand dug up from below my fingers, changing its shape with each movement but leaving no lasting memory behind.

My hand clenched the sand as I lifted it up in defiance. I had lived my life to leave a lasting legacy, refusing to accept the fate that befalls all men. Yet, I couldn't help but think how this legacy of mine was like the sand in my fist. No matter how hard I tried to keep it there, the sand slowly seeped through the cracks between each finger and bounced off my arm before falling back to the beach below. As I relaxed my grip, the sand fell at a quicker pace until there was nothing left. The grains settled where it fell, forgetting how it had been lifted up and ending back from whence it came. I could not change the flow of time, not now, not ever.

As I began to view my life in a new perspective, I couldn't look away from the reflection that my mind was giving me. I felt stiff, unable to move as the thoughts came through. My life had all been for me and my personal glory, with

no thought of a mortal death that was soon to come. The ocean waves crashing into the beach and returning back to the seas only brought me a sober reminder of the eternal cycle of life and death on this earth.

As the sun began to fade in the sky, the breeze no longer provided a warming comfort, only a cold and deathly chill that passed through my bones, continuing on its predetermined path. The warmth that once brought life soon found its release, as it could never win against the coldness hiding below the surface, waiting for its time to come.

Time did not grant me an exception to its continuous cycle, but rather moved faster with each passing day, slipping past me as quickly as the sand from my very hand. The beach stretched beyond the horizon with no end and no beginning. My thoughts began to understand how lonely, afraid, and tired life was when no one else was around. I had gained all I wanted in my short existence, living as one with no thought of an afterlife or consequences to my actions. The retirement I spent my entire life working towards was not what I had envisioned. The accumulation of wealth did not make me happy, but instead it brought an overwhelming bitterness. I had given up everything for this very moment; my friends, my faith, my very soul. Now, as time neared its very end, I had nothing left. There was no laughter, no comfort, and no joy. All that kept me company was my thoughts of regret.

Why did the beach bring such an emptiness to my soul? I pondered the question until darkness wrapped around me like a cold and desolate blanket.

UNSTABLE GROUND

This was perfection. Sanctification had done its work and my sinful past was gone. I was the most modest, the most devout, and the most knowledgeable Christian amongst my peers. People came to me for advice and the wisdom that I shared. I was a mentor to hundreds and a saint to thousands. The humblest of the humble.

If only all people could be like me, then this world would be a better place and God's kingdom would reign supreme.

I sat on my perch, overlooking the city, a stable rock made out of my own skill and handiwork. Even God would be proud of how high I had reached. This place up in the sky is where I looked down upon others and judged them for underachieving, making life-altering mistakes, or repeat offenses from a lack of discipline.

Though, I had no time to deal with their issues or fix them. My job in life was to be an example of godly perfection to anyone able or willing to strive for it. This is how I spent my time, up on my perch, too high for anyone to reach me, too high for any dirt to get on my clothes, and too high to be bothered with the heathens below. Let them look up to me and see, to see what they could become if they only believed in themselves.

It was at this very moment, at the apex of my godliness, that the rock I built began to give way. My perch felt unstable and untenable, but how? But why? I had done everything right and built this rock and foundation to perfection. I couldn't believe what was happening as the perch failed to hold me up and the fear of falling grew heavy on me. I lifted my hands to the heavens, asking God to keep me stable.

The answer came, but it was not what I expected. Lightning bolts struck the perch from the heavens and giant cracks formed on the rock below my feet. As I

fell down from the shattered perch, I saw everything I had built break into pieces. It had taken me decades to build what I had through discipline and hard work, but now it was all gone in a matter of seconds. Why would God do this to his most faithful follower?

I awoke with a shock, laying on top of the rubble that used to be my personal tower and perch. In an instant, I had gone from the highest point in the sky to the lowest part of the ground, covered in dirt, grime, and shame. How did this happen, I thought to myself? What did I do wrong? Did God not love me for what I had become?

Unable to comprehend what had happened, I could only look on as the lowly began to circle around the destruction of my tower. What did I miss? Had I not worked my entire life to be where I was through discipline, hard work, and prayer? Why had my perch been destroyed? There were plenty of others with more faults than my own whose perches still stood high in the sky. I didn't understand my predicament, my sin, my faults. Where did I go wrong? My whole life had been dedicated to perfection and godliness.

It was in my brokenness that the wind started blowing, bringing with it a gentle breeze that spoke in a whisper. "Follow me," it said.

"But I am!" I cried out loud. "I did everything I was supposed to."

As I spoke my defense, a vision came to me. A silent Jesus before his accusers; a silent Jesus who never stopped serving his disciples; a silent Jesus who washed his disciples' feet; a silent Jesus who would do anything to put others before himself; a silent Jesus who descended from heaven from his perch in the sky to show us the way. The vision revealed how a humble heart does not think of humbleness.

I must've forgotten the example of Jesus. In my pride, in my selfishness, I had put myself above others and had made myself a god in Jesus' place. It had taken his love for me to break my perch and expose my sin for what it was, the sin of pride, the sin of man from the very beginning which had crept its way back into my life. I had forgotten to keep Jesus as the center of my faith. My love for others had disappeared and been replaced by a self-righteousness and a deep love for myself and the works I had done.

Jesus had finally chosen to oppose me and the pride that had built within. Oh how my fall shook me and all those who had seen me up in the sky. "Leave me alone in my shame!" I cried into the wind. But the wind was gone as soon as it had arrived. No sooner had it gone than the stones of my pride began to crumble to dust around me. I felt my body settle on solid ground as the rocks vanished like the sand of the desert. It did not blow away, but stayed as a reminder; letting me know to never build another perch, but to stay true to Jesus' example and serve the lost and needy.

My two feet had to stay on the ground, I knew. No perch could ever save me or help me. The only goodness came from knowing Jesus and serving his will. But what if I tried to build a tower once again, I thought? No, I told myself, I wouldn't let that happen and I trusted that God would not either. I would remember my savior and what he accomplished by giving up his throne and taking my place on the cross.

THE PANIC ATTACK

It was my second panic attack of the week. No matter what I did, the feeling of a crushing weight coming in from all sides never let go or subsided. Any chance that I could escape from reality helped alleviate the stress which kept building up like a kettle hitting the critical boiling point. It was a constant pain in my chest that was a sign from my body that everything was not okay and that something had to change.

But what?

And how?

The questions lingered in my mind as a walked into my room. It was here that I could hide myself from all that was going on in my life. But this time, no matter what I did, I could not stop my mind from thinking about it. And then that's when the second panic attack hit me.

The walls surrounding me began to shrink in and it made me feel as if I would be crushed where I sat. The first wall that started to move inwards was the one in front of me. I could see it now, representing the need to support my family financially. A daughter was to be born to us and all I could think about was how to support her without additional income. It was my responsibility to provide and there was no time to look for a new job or a way to ask for a raise. Everything we needed to buy kept going up in costs each year and still my income was stagnant, unable to provide anything more than the necessities we had now. What about baby clothes, formula, and car seat? Everything that we had to get required money and the thought of raising a girl in a world without all she needed overwhelmed me.

The wall to my right was my job. It was the second wall to begin moving towards me, ready to crush the very life from my body. The demands had increased and with several colleagues leaving in a short time period, and I was left to meet all the deadlines. I was promised help and a raise, but neither was coming and with each day of work, my body grew tenser, trying to cope with a job not meant for just one person. I felt stuck with no way out and a job whose demands took all the energy from my day. No one can live under this type of pressure for long, and my body finally cracked under the pressure.

I tried looking to my left, but it didn't help and only made it worse. This wall started to move closer faster than the other two. My dad was with Parkinson's disease and needed daily assistance. We were the only ones capable to care for him after my mother had passed away. Caring for my immediate family was hard enough, but the pressure of a parent who needed daily attention only made things that much more difficult. The daily stress was enough by itself, but now it added on top of everything else that was going on. There was too little time in the day and nothing left for myself.

I began to cry, feeling like my heart was going to jump out from the chest as it beat uncontrollably. There was no mechanism, no way to stop the pain from subsiding. I was caught between the walls of the room, the door lost from sight, and the last wall closing slowly behind me. This wall was the one I wanted to evade from thinking about most of all. Our marriage was slowly eroding as we constantly fought and struggled to make ends meet. The stress was taking its toll on both of us, and I didn't know how to fix our marriage before it fell apart. I didn't know how long we could hold on together before the pain and stress tore us from each other. I couldn't go on alone, but turning things around meant finding solutions to the problems overwhelming our lives.

It was beyond comprehension, beyond what any human should have to deal with in life. I was at my wits end. I had no way out, no way to push against the walls that looked to crush both body and soul. All I could do was try my best to control the beatings of my heart, to breath in and breath out, but it only prolonged the inevitable. The walls grew closer and closer.

I was left with only one option, one way out from this panic attack that threatened to end my life. I cried out to God, asking for help, praying for only a little relief to aid in my greatest time of need. I had no other recourse but to trust in God, even if I didn't know that help would come. I prayed, "I believe, but help

my unbelief!" If he could just show a little mercy towards me, then I could make it through today.

As soon as I prayed, I began to feel a sense of peace coming in waves. It emanated from a hymn that could be heard in the room as it played through the notes. I started to focus on this and sang along to its melodious tune. My heart began to beat normally and the walls slowly moved away from me. It didn't remove all my stress, but gave me just enough to carry on through the day and to stop the panic attack that had set in. It was God's way to show me his love and that he had given me the tool I needed when the stress and anxiety started to overwhelm me again.

If I could focus on a hymn and sing along, it would help get my mind away from everything going on around me. I thanked God for his help, and started to slowly regain a sense of myself. Nothing would be easy, but for the first time in a long time, I began to feel that I could make it through to the other side. I just had to take one day at a time and trust in God along the way. He would help me through.

WEAK AND HELPLESS

Weak and helpless I try to stand
Unable to lift up my sun-scorched hand
Hopelessness fills me in this lifeless land
Surrounded by ghosts in a desert of sand

This life has become too much to bear
No one to help me, no pain to share
Sadness has passed, no more hurt, nor a care
My eyes have run dry, no not even a tear

I was tired of this life that had become an eternal hell
May the devil take my soul that I wanted to sell
In my anguish and shame, I heard a sound I tried to quell
A voice from heaven, clear and soft from what I could tell

Speaking of a love so great with a caring tone
It would not relent or leave me alone
The message of a savior slain broke my heart of stone
How God stepped down from His heavenly throne

I finally let go of my sin and shame
No longer caring about any pointless fame
All I had sought before felt embarrassing and lame
Replaced by a new life, filled with an eternal flame

THE HOUSE (PART 4) – THE BEDROOM

Now that my finances were in order, I wanted to get back out into the dating scene. Time to put my effort into chasing girls instead of chasing material goods, I thought to myself. Jesus had helped with the finances anyway, and with a better budget, I had the freedom to spend it on women. I had broken up from a long-term relationship prior to meeting Jesus, and now that I started to think about it, I missed having a girlfriend by my side. The loneliness that began to creep back into my mind kept making me believe I was missing something important. I had felt content with Jesus, but as time went by, he just wasn't enough. I mean, he usually just sat there silently, looking at me to do something. It was borderline creepy, but maybe he just was the silent type.

Still, the quietness that came to me at night, allowed for my mind to wander. It drifted back to the days of my ex. How she had fulfilled me and all the desires I had. If only I could go back into the dating scene and find someone special again. I needed someone to replace her so I could remember the good times and keep me occupied. But I wasn't ready to commit to anyone through marriage, I was too young for that.

I soon realized that the Christian values could be used for my benefit when it came to dating women. I had almost doubted myself for letting Jesus move in until I realized how it would benefit me with other areas of my life. Women seemed drawn to me just by treating them like I didn't care. It was a common practice in my old days, but now that I got Jesus, I had a better solution. Finding a woman to replace my last one should be simple. I must be every woman's dream based on my new set of virtues and my ability to stand above other men. Let them come to me, I thought, then I'll catch them in my net.

There was one main hurdle that I had to overcome. This came about when I first tried to bring a new girl to my house. Having to let the girl know I had a "roommate" didn't quite go over so well. I played it off the best I could at the beginning, but eventually they would be weirded out by Jesus' perfection. Then it would all go downhill, and the girls would leave me as they couldn't handle letting me have him sit around in my house. The girls noticed the double life that I tried to live, and that Jesus acted like a sort of "dad" that kept an eye on me and what I did.

This one night out in the city, I finally found this girl who made me laugh. We were able to talk all night and I felt this strong emotional connection. I believed she had real potential, and I wanted to keep her for as long as I could. Though, as usual, Jesus became the biggest problem hindering the relationship. She was very blunt about her thoughts on him and made it seem like I would have to choose between the two. She didn't care about wanting to get to know Jesus. So, of course, it put me at a crossroads. I thought, maybe if I hid Jesus from her, she wouldn't notice. It made me think of some excuse or way to hide Jesus from her for the time being, at least until the relationship was stable enough and she would be okay with having him around.

The idea came to me later the next day. My house had this back entrance that would lead to a small room right next to my bedroom. The look that Jesus would give me, and her, meant that avoiding the front entrance seemed like the smartest thing to do. Besides, normally I wouldn't bring a girl to my house during the day and I didn't want to bother Jesus late at night anyway, so why should I disturb him? I did not want this to be a hindrance for the life I wanted to live. Privacy is important, and Jesus shouldn't be listening in to our conversations or see our physical intimacy, even though I felt guilty trying to hide it.

For the time being, using the back door turned into a win/win situation for me. I would not feel uncomfortable by the look Jesus gave me, and I did not have to explain to her why Jesus was still at my house. I just had to keep up this long enough for her to be comfortable whenever she would see Jesus. This whole issue would be resolved soon enough, or at least this is what I believed. Yet, for some reason, the thought of living a double life kept me from truly enjoying the

relationship and it was hard to keep up the facade. It was as if Jesus had this way to make me feel guilty even though I didn't see him with her. I had to continuously try and ignore these thoughts in my head as soon as they appeared.

I wanted my new girlfriend to fill the void that the last one had vacated. Instead, every morning I felt worse than I had the day before. The temporary happiness and love from my new girlfriend did not heal me. It only felt as if the scab had been ripped off and the wound grew worse each and every day. As the weekends continued, the emotional highs began to subside and the emptiness I had was once again beginning to appear, despite having this new girlfriend. This feeling of despair grew inside of me. Why was my new girlfriend not the answer I had hoped she would be? Why could I not have her and Jesus? Didn't Jesus want to make me happy?

It became a viscous cycle that dragged me further down, just like a drug that never satisfied. I did not come out feeling that I was cured, rather that the medication was not strong enough. The thing is, I wanted my girlfriend to cure me, to fix and fill the void in my heart. Yet, the new prescription I gave myself only added to the emptiness. It was as if I already had the prescription with Jesus, but I refused to use it. I wanted this girl to make me feel alive and happy, but I knew deep down that she could not accept me for my convictions, and I could never fully commit to her. Sadness turned into anger and I didn't understand why I felt this way.

It was during one of these mornings where I finally decided to ask Jesus why I felt the way that I did. He pointed to the Bible, but I scoffed at him. "The view of relationships in the Bible is outdated," I said, "how could it speak to us in this day and age? You should be able to date anyone you want. There are no rules to relationships that can help me, and besides, sex is just a physical thing and it doesn't affect you long term. I should be able to date any girl I want, Christian or not." I used every argument I could all at once that had been sold to me by the secular society. But Jesus seemed unperturbed by my solid reasoning.

He cut through all my excuses and arguments and only said, "Then why do you feel the way that you do?"

The anger began to boil up inside of me once again. That anger I got from not having the fulfillment I required in life. I was almost ready to let Jesus hear my wrath, to let out my pain and hurt that had come with the actions I took. Though, for some reason, I stopped myself. I walked away to a quiet place. My thoughts whirled in my mind as I began to think more clearly with the rage and anger subsiding. Why did the depression and despair I felt grow worse after dating this new girlfriend and the freedom I had seemed to disappear? I was seeking to fill a hole in my heart with this woman, but like a puzzle piece, her square peg didn't fit into the round whole, no matter how hard I tried. Deep down I knew this, but I had been blinded to it because of my physical desires and lust that clouded my judgment.

Another few weeks went by, but I couldn't shake the feelings I had in my mind. Then the ultimatum came. I guess it was inevitable, but nonetheless, I knew it would eventually come. My girlfriend decided to come over unexpectedly, but not to the back entrance, instead she came to the front. As I was in the shower at that time, Jesus answered the door for me. The shock, horror, and all the other emotions that must've shown on her face, were probably there all at once. When I came down and noticed what happened, this long and awkward silence ensued. I wanted to hide under the carpet, but as much as I entertained the idea, the carpet was just not a good enough deception. I needed a trap door under the carpet, I thought to myself.

As I began to think of all possible excuses that I could use, none that made any sense came to mind. My quick wit had finally failed me for the last time. How could I get myself out of this mess? I looked at Jesus, who only looked back in silence, but with that smile he had when he saw someone new come over. It's like he expected me to tell everyone who came over about how important he was to me, which was kind of selfish. I mean, I'd much rather talk about myself.

Anyway, so here I was, having to face the consequences of my decisions. My girlfriend felt offended and hurt that I had hid Jesus. She had told me that she did not want anything to do with him, but now she saw how Jesus was all up in my personal business. For one, she was not happy that I lied to her, but more than that, she didn't like that I had hid my faith from her. So, after some fighting, or a lot of fighting, depending on how you count time, she gave me this ultimatum. She wanted me to get rid of Jesus or she would leave me for good. That wasn't fair I thought, I should be able to keep both. She stormed out of the house when I told her I couldn't do it, that Jesus was too important as a resident in my house.

As I sat down in the living room, all dejected and feeling sad for myself, Jesus decided that it was a great time to break the silence. His words were short, but always full of wisdom. Any argument at this point would have left me in defeat, but it was the one statement He picked that mattered the most.

His words I would not forget, even to this day. He said, "Do you not see, do you not understand? I am all you need. Seek first the Kingdom of Heaven, and all else will be given to you. Do not seek in others from what only I can give." He paused and with a sadness in his eyes, continued. "They are my daughters that you are lying too, daughters whom I love, even the ones who are walking the wrong path."

The words tore through me like a knife through melted butter.

I never realized the choices I had made, never understood the consequences of my actions. I had looked at women as an object to be worshiped, to be used, to fill the hole in my heart, and not as something precious. My selfishness refused to see beyond my own pain and into the heart of another. If they are his daughters, I thought…should they not be seen as my sisters?

The thought of my actions, the way I had treated this girl and all the ones before her, began to flood through my mind. I couldn't look Jesus in the eye, I felt unclean, evil, and dirty. All it took was a few words and my entire worldview shattered before me. I was left with an ultimatum by her, but now I see that the choice wasn't hard, heck, it was a situation I shouldn't even have put myself in.

I started to remember what the girlfriend I had told me. She had come from a recently broken relationship and was seeking the same thing I had, to fill the hole in her heart, to find someone to meet the needs that she wanted filled. I looked past this because what I cared about more was as her body, not her soul. She had left with a broken heart and did not see Jesus as the one that could heal her. I had looked past her pain because of my inability to see beyond my own short-term desires.

The pain and hurt that was in the world around me was real. I, just like everyone else, thought sex was a way to fill a void in the heart. That the passions of the flesh were just physical. I knew this could not be true anymore, not after what I had gone through and the words of Jesus which cut into my soul.

I slowly took the key to my bedroom and gave it to Jesus. It would take time for me to heal from this pain and grow, but one thing I knew, I couldn't view the women I was with or the relationships I had the same way as before. My willingness to let Jesus hold me accountable while I was dating a girl was a beginning, I knew. Maybe, I thought, I should hold off until the right time to do so.

The road would not be an easy one, and I was glad that I still had one place of solace left to go. The last key burned in my pocket, begging me to follow its call to the basement.

THE GIANT SHADOW

It was only a quick glance, at first, but it didn't stop there. An image on the wall of a building, a short scene in a movie, a picture inside a magazine. In the beginning, I had thought nothing of it; however, something had stirred inside of me each time that my eyes caught the object of my fascination. My body responded with feelings of pleasure, of desire, of lust. I didn't know what to make of it at the beginning, but I found myself thirsting and wanting more. It was a hunger that quickly grew into an irresistible force, as if it had been there all along, just waiting for the right time to show itself.

My curiosity to these newfound feelings meant that the glances weren't enough as the images began to sear into my brain, reminding me that they were there and available. I soon found myself noticing more images, and I lingered for a few seconds, and then seconds turned into minutes, and minutes into… well, more time than I had planned. Once I found that the sensations of pleasure were addicting, the lusts of my flesh took over. The urges that grew inside needed to be fed and I quickly gave what it required so it could grow and become a mind of its own. It became a giant shadow that followed me around wherever I went, turning women into objects and beauty into sexuality. It was much easier to just accept the shadow as a necessary part of me rather than trying to fight against it. This way the urges could easily be quenched and my morality only slightly compromised.

As time went on, I found myself depressed and empty when my appetite wasn't being satisfied from the images feeding into my brain with continuous pleasure. The giant shadow would remind me that if I only experienced something new, something more pleasurable, then I would feel greater than ever before. It pushed me deeper and further into my lusts than I had ever imagined going before. The problem was that these new experiences, which felt great and pleasurable in

the moment, did not make me feel happier than before. It wasn't this part that bothered me the most, it was the promises that never went fulfilled and had become a hollow echo chamber of lies.

I tried to find ways to live without these thoughts permeating my mind, but the giant shadow had infiltrated every part of my life, pushing me deeper into its dark embrace. It changed how I viewed any woman that walked into my vision. I would associate with others who thought the same so I could justify the pleasures of the flesh, but something deep inside my soul screamed that this wasn't right.

Years passed by as the chains grew thicker around me, feeding off of me to satisfy the appetite of the giant shadow. Nothing changed and nothing released me from the prison of my own design. It wasn't until one fateful evening after going further into my fantasy dreams of lust than ever before that everything came crashing to a head. I sat in my room feeling empty, depressed, and utterly lonely. A sense of tiredness with the same feelings that I couldn't escape overwhelmed me and forced me into action. I felt this urge; this need to get rid of this giant shadow that had become an extension of my very own body.

As I left my apartment, the giant shadow followed me close behind. I started to run faster and faster, but I couldn't shake it off me or lose it no matter the amount of light that was directed its way. I finally turned into an alley, not realizing that it was a dead end until the wall swallowed up my vision. Running had gotten me nowhere and I was desperate, unwilling to give up. I had to act now.

I screamed at the giant shadow. "Leave me alone! I've had enough of your lies and empty promises!" It began to slowly move, separating itself from me and taking the shape of a tall and muscular human. Its mouth formed into an evil grin and its eyes glowed as two rubies in hollowed sockets. The giant shadow spoke no words, but it didn't have to. I knew its intentions as if it were my own.

The only way for me to get through this was to battle my way out. I took my fighting stance and prepared for what was to come. It waited for me to move, confidence brimming within its smile. I wanted to hit that smirk right off of its face and so a ran forward, cocking my arm back to swing a nasty right hook in its face, the chains dragging around me.

It felt like hours had gone by, but I knew it was much shorter than that. I could taste the blood in my mouth as I tried to pull myself back up from the ground. It was not the pain of the hit, nor the ringing in my head that made it real. It was the blood pouring from my broken off tooth that brought the taste of defeat.

Resting with one knee on the ground, I tried to regain my senses. The fight wasn't over, but I could see no path towards victory. My opponent was too strong, knew all my weaknesses, and constantly stayed one step ahead. It was as if it had studied my every move better than I knew myself. I spit the tooth onto the ground where it lay covered in blood and saliva. The empty socket quickly filled up with blood, bringing back the metallic taste once again.

It would be better for me to stay on the ground, admit defeat, and forget that the fight was ever present, ever real, and ever foreboding. All I could do was give up and go back to being a slave to the giant shadow for the rest of my life. Without a chance of victory, would there ever be another option? Was it worth the effort to keep fighting and to keep myself from the inevitable defeat that my opponent desired?

I spat more blood on the ground in defiance. All my life I believed in myself that I could conquer anything I put my mind to; that I had the strength to defeat whatever came my way. So why not this giant shadow? Why was there this feeling of inevitable defeat and that I could not fight it any longer? The shadow must've slowly removed my ability to fight for the freedom that existed beyond the darkness of the alley. I could sense it, but I couldn't grasp it.

The giant shadow wanted to keep me bound in chains, to bring me back to the dungeon of my lusts and desires in which I had wanted to escape. Yes, the chains. How could I forget? They were slowing me down and stopping me from truly making the fight an even one. It held me back and kept me from being released out of the bonds that had systematically pulled me down such a dark path. Escaping the dungeon wasn't good enough, not if the giant shadow knew how to capture me once again. Its smirk knew that the inevitable result of my efforts would result in defeat. And its mighty blows proved this to be true. Bondage is what it sought; hopelessness is what it brought.

I wanted to cry out to God, but would he answer? I pushed his help aside long ago when I thought that my own strength would protect me when the time came. How wrong I was! I was on my knees, spitting blood, struggling to survive because of my own pride and immoral desires. I knew what I had to do, but the humbleness it required is what held me back.

The inner struggle made it difficult to think, but an answer had to come before I took another blow from the giant shadow. I knew that it was now or never to break free because my courage would fail me after this bitter loss. One thing was sure, I did not want to go back to the dungeon of darkness that I came from and only God had the power to truly set me free from the chains that bound me. Without him, I had no hope to defeat the giant shadow which towered menacingly over me.

I cried out to God for help with my head on the ground and arms stretched out. I expected a final blow from the giant shadow, a final hit to send me into unconsciousness.

But it never came.

Instead a bright light showed through between the buildings of the alley from up above. It quickly defeated the giant shadow with its penetrating light, broke my chains, and brought me energy to stand once again. The fight was won in an instant and Jesus stood in its stead. He conquered my sin and broke the chains that had me bound to the giant shadow. With my immoral perversions removed, I could once again see the power of the cross and the strength it gave.

A SECOND CHANCE

It was an unplanned trip, but a much needed one. The mountains felt like my home away from home and I knew the trails like the back of my hand. No matter how much the world changed around me, the natural scenery always remained constant. The stones were older than time itself and stretched farther than the eye could see while the trees stood ageless amongst the rocky terrain. The canyon where I spent most of my time felt like it was my very own backyard. Coming here never grew old and hiking these trails brought me much needed rest and peace of mind. It was my solace, a place that I could go and be one with nature, reflecting on all the things that life brought my way. And this time I needed it more than ever before.

I was living in an ever-expanding bubble and it was bound to burst at any point. Few could carry the burden that sat in my heart, but I was set on keeping it secret for as long as I could. You see, I had my wife of ten years, but also this young and energetic college student who made me feel alive like never before. A small part, deep inside of me, knew that this was wrong, but my self-discipline had quickly evaporated to the irresistible smile and wooing of this young woman. What man on earth does not crave to be wanted? It was simply that I had taken it a step too far.

I knew not how to deal with this dilemma. I could not leave my wife, but how could I confront her with what I have done? Exposing it would cause more pain than I could bear to see on her face. One thing was for certain, and that was a need to end it with the other woman. But I knew not how and I did not know if I had the will power to undertake such a task. I had to get out and away from it all, to escape.

Walking through the hilly terrain quickly grew burdensome. I stopped to look around and for some reason I found myself having wandered into an area that I

don't remember ever venturing before. It must've been a new animal trail that had led me astray. I shook my head for having let my mind lose focus, but there was no doubt in my mind that I could eventually find my way back.

It wasn't until close to dark that I realized something wasn't right. I was completely and utterly lost. I hadn't brought anything to stay through the night and I soon became worried. There was a sparse crop of trees close by that provided shade from the setting sun and a smooth fallen tree that looked sturdy enough to sit on. It seemed better than any other spot I could find, and I quickly made my way over to it. It was a sunny day and hotter than usual, and the energy from the hike had worn me out. Survival started to become a factor more than any worry of my life back home. Untwisting the top to my water canister, I took a good long drink to quench my thirsty and tired body. I needed to think and orient myself so I could find my way back to the car.

As I relaxed on the fallen tree, I saw movement coming out from beneath it and froze. A large black snake, bigger than I had ever seen in the area before, emerged from under the tree. It circled by my foot before moving onto it. I didn't instantly react, but instead became fascinated by its glittering and shiny skin. As it began to wrap around my foot and slither up my leg, my mind tried to tell me to flee, to quickly run away. But instead of moving and seeking safer ground, I let my defenses down, thinking that it was a friendly snake that wouldn't harm me.

What I thought and hoped for was wrong. It had quickly gained my trust through its movements, but it wasn't my friend and its intentions were bent on evil. As it got closer to my hand, the venomous and devious snake struck out and bit me. At my very weakest, it had struck hard and fast, its poison spreading quickly through my veins and straight into my beating heart. The snake's darkened soul became clear and its intentions known, and it soon disappeared where it came from, leaving me weak and unable to move.

Shock and fear kept me from moving. There was very little time to take any action as my muscles started to stiffen, leaving me with only a short time left on this earth. I knew that there was no hope for survival and regret began to replace fear.

I was a mess, a full rotten mess. My soulmate, my dearest love, and the one whom I promised to spend eternity with, it was her that I betrayed, and now she will never know the truth. I had traded her faith by lusting after another and the snake had meted out the justice that I deserved. The only thing left in this life for me is regret. Bitten by passion and left for dead.

How did I end up this way?

All the choices along the way had led me deeper into sin. I began to pinpoint all the mistakes that were made and wondering how life would've been different.

How could I have betrayed the very words that I promised during the marriage ceremony? It was supposed to be a deep and lasting covenant, but it stood broken and shattered. Deserving was my death, and how sad and lonely it would be.

It cut me to the heart.

I was not Judas Iscariot; I did not sell Jesus for thirty pieces of silver. But deep inside I felt just the same. My sin had been another stake into the flesh of Jesus' hands and feet. I wouldn't hang myself like Judas did, but the bite from the snake would have the same effect and my life was truly over. I couldn't be a leader of anyone. No courage or strength to stand up for all that was true.

Maybe, just maybe, I could be given a second chance. What if what Jesus said was true? That even with my betrayal that there was a chance of forgiveness? Oh, that was my hope. I wanted forgiveness for my mistakes; I wanted a second chance! Oh Lord, please grant me this one wish, I prayed. This one favor to be restored. Satan is putting me down, but he will not win. He will not sift me like sand and leave me in regret from my mistakes and betrayal.

Some semblance of a last plea to God entered my mind. I knew only minutes remained of my life and I had to repent and try to make things right.

"Please Father!" I prayed. "Give me a second chance to redeem the wrong I have done. Bring me up from the ashes and restore me from my shame and guilt. I will follow You and I will live for You for the rest of my life on earth. Just give me this chance to do what is right. Please restore me in Your great mercy." And then everything went dark.

It was the chirping of the birds that woke me. The sun was rising in the east and its rays shone brightly on my face. I looked up to the heavens and gave a silent prayer of thankfulness. What lied in front of me was a road filled with pain and sorrow, but I knew what had to be done. There was no reason to wait as time was never going to be on my side. God had mercy on me and it was not because of my goodness. I had created a ripple effect of decisions that would cause pain and heartache to my wife, family, and anyone this adultery affected. Picking up the pieces could take years, decades and the consequences would last a lifetime.

I get up to leave, and the trail home quickly opened up in front of me and even though it was a narrow road, its path was straight and true. My reconciliation with God was only the beginning of the journey in front of me.

THE DOUBLE-EDGED SWORD

For the word of God is living and active, sharper than any two-edged sword, piercing to the division of soul and of spirit, of joints and of marrow, and discerning the thoughts and intentions of the heart.
Hebrews 4:12

My mouth opened in a silent scream as the double-edged sword found its mark with ease, piercing through my flesh and straight to the heart. I had fought day and night against my foe, refusing to give in, even when winning had seemed futile. The earth below me felt cold to the touch as I lay with my arms out wide. The sword sapped away all my remaining energy and left me gasping for air. No more could I defend against the blows of my enemy; no longer could I fight for my life. I was pinned to the earth with nowhere to run or hide. I welcomed the strike, an end to the misery that the last few days had brought. The double-edged blade knew its mark and its strike was true.

The pain of the blade was sharp and real, yet the wound drew no blood. It cut to the core of my heart, but I could still feel the pulse of life-giving blood throughout my body. All I could do was be still and wait for the coldness of death to overtake me.

It never came.

The double-edged sword began to glow and pulsate, imitating the beats of my heart, providing a warmth that grew in contrast to the cold earth below. A moment of panic started to build up as I lay pinned to the ground, not knowing what to expect or what would come next. All my struggles had amounted to nothing. There

was no hope left to accomplish anything out of my own power. I closed my eyes and tried one more thing. My mind sent a silent prayer fervently to God for the first time in years, asking to be rescued and for one more chance at life.

A sudden stream of emotions began flooding through me as the glow of the sword had unlocked something hidden deep inside. It took over my soul like a bolt of lightning from the clouds above. The pain, the hurt, the tears that I caused to the one whom I loved the most, overwhelmed me. The realization of what I had done, all the yelling, abuse, and pain was from a place of darkness which had festered and grown in my heart. I did not see it and I could not understand it, not until I was pierced through the heart by this…this double-edged sword. It carried the truth of who I was straight into the deepest part of my soul and bringing with it the reality of what I had become. It crept up from my heart and into my mind as it overwhelmed my thoughts and emotions.

I knew now that my selfishness and pride had created barriers that blocked anything from penetrating and breaking the darkness inside. I ruined what had been the only good thing left in my life because of the consequences from my actions.

Tears streamed down my face as I sought to claw the memories from my mind. The sword brought conviction and a realization that had been hidden and left for dead. It pierced, not my heart, but the darkness surrounding it. It struck deep into my soul, not to finish me, but to redeem the brokenness.

I began to understand that the pain which I felt was not from the double-edged sword, it was my own sin and shame that was being exposed. I hid my pain into the deepest recesses of my heart, hoping that it would never be released or exposed to anyone. But there it had festered, grown beyond its small box, and affecting my life and relationship with others.

As the double-edged sword removed itself from my heart, it took with it the darkness that had blinded me for so long. I was left broken, but with a newfound hope. Freed from the chains of sin, but vulnerable and exposed. I was in a place of remorse but not without strength to continue on. I knew what I had to do, though the path to redemption would not be an easy one.

THE BETRAYER

"Nooo!" I cried, "Not my baby!" The words settled on deaf ears, for I knew that no one could change the judgement given by God. It wasn't long after that Nathan, the prophet, had left that everyone began to filter out from the throne room. It left me empty, shattered, and broken. I had never felt more alone than any time before. No one dared to stay and console me after what was prophesied about my sinful actions.

No longer did people see me as a sinless man, but a betrayer and selfish king. The trust which was built up had now been broken and shattered in front of everyone.

I had reached out to the prophet, asking, pleading, hoping that he would tell me that the words spoken were not true and that God would have mercy on my son. If only I could go back in time, to repent from my sins, and to stop what I had done. I had been a coward, a ruthless traitor to cover up such a great sin. My best friend I killed and his wife I took in greed. All for lust and passion for another which was not mine to take.

To think that I could hide this from God himself. For I now know my transgressions, and my sin is ever before me. It is against God I have sinned and done what is evil in his sight. I was to represent him to his people and all the nations around, but I failed miserably.

Now, now the verdict had been given and my judgment complete. What I had done in secret, God exposed in daylight to all around. I could hide my transgressions no longer as it was laid out bare to all the people of Israel. My unborn son, conceived of adultery, would not taste the life of this world for long. A baby lost, a life for a life. How could I ever live with myself or even be king over these people, to show my face in public? I, chosen by God to be king, turned

into the biggest betrayer of all. I had everything I ever wanted, but I still looked for more. My eyes deceived me, my flesh desired, and I took what was forbidden, just like Adam and Eve in the Garden of Eden. I was born in iniquity, and in sin did my mother conceive me.

I took my sorrows and sadness to my private room, unable to speak, unable to respond to anyone, not even my servants. All I could do was weep for the child yet born, filled with the guilt and grief of what I had done. I had become a stumbling block for the nation, a point of shame for those who were more righteous than I. Maybe, through my prayers, God would spare the unborn baby, to spare that which was done in sin. I knew, oh, how I knew, that God was compassionate and merciful, forgiving and just. All He had done through me was more than I could ever hope. Now this, this disappointment, that had caused a great sin and righteous judgment.

I deserved this, I knew. But I would still pray and hope that God would show his great mercy on me once again and to wash away the wickedness that my hands had done. That one day, one day, he would send his Son as promised, to take on my sin and shame. This promise was all I had left to live on. Without this, I could not go on.

May God show mercy on my baby, to bring him to the place of paradise before my time. That my sin would be covered and my life freed from the shackles that hold me down. May God carry my shame and my guilt, to have mercy on my soul. May he fulfill his promise in the years to come.

Purge me with hyssop, oh God, and I shall be clean. Wash me, and I shall be whiter than snow. Let me hear joy and gladness once again and let the bones that you have broken rejoice. Hide your face from my sins, and blot out all my iniquities. Create in me a clean heart, O God, and renew a right spirit within me. Cast me not away from your presence, and take not your Holy Spirit from me. Restore to me the joy of your salvation and uphold me with a willing spirit.

Let the nations sing of God's goodness and to praise him as Lord. Teach people your ways O God, to look beyond my sin, and to a perfect, sinless Messiah that is to come.

A PRAYER TO GOD

O God, you know my folly;
the wrongs I have done are not hidden from you.
Let not those who hope in you be put to shame through me,
O Lord God of hosts;
let not those who seek you be brought to dishonor through me,
O God of Israel.
-Psalm 69:5-6

O God, you know all of my mistakes, failures, and shortcomings. Nothing is hidden and everything I have done wrong to those around me is seen by you. Above all else, I have sinned against you by following my own path in life. My sins and failures have been kept in darkness for far too long and I have lived thinking that maybe, just maybe this one lie would not be counted against me. But I could never keep that promise. It would happen again and again and again. I lived believing that if I was my own god, I could change my mistakes by doing good to others.

How foolish I was all this time! How can I hide my faults by trying to do good? O God, you see everything and know everything.

How could I believe that the darkness in my heart would not be seen by your holy light? That I live life believing I had something to lose, and this loss would be the nakedness of my soul poured out and seen by those around me. How much I wanted to hide behind my lies and deceit, O Lord, and all those desires and temptations that Satan was sending my way each and every day. Oh, how foolish I was to think that you could not see through my soul!

Let not those who hope in you be put to shame through me, O Lord God. Let those who see me, see you! I pray that my walk through this life is not lived in

darkness. That I trust you and be humbled in my faults so that your glory can shine that much brighter through me. Help me to be the witness that you want me to be so that others who believe in you can see the strength that you have given me. Let me uplift and encourage my brothers and sisters in Christ by living a humble and faith-filled life. Give me the wisdom to know the difference in the choices I make and live in obedience to your Word.

Let not those who seek you be brought to dishonor through me, O God. Let me be the witness that you want me to be. Let me reach out with love and be filled with the Holy Spirit. Let me not seek to judge others and instead show them the joy that only you can bring. Help me to listen to your voice and be a person of integrity that will allow your life to shine into those who seek the Truth. Only with your guidance can I help others turn to you and to understand the joy that awaits them in eternity.

MY DAUGHTER

Her eyes welled up with tears as she tugged at the strings of my heart. All she wanted was for me to lift her up and hold her close, but something held me back. But why now? It was something I had done a million times before. The innocence in her eyes could not fathom or understand this pain that I carried deep inside, scarring my inner being. It was the part of me that laid silent behind a thin layer of ice for so long and now was an overwhelming feeling of depression and sadness.

She did not know or comprehend how she had become both my love and my pain. My joy and my sorrow. My happiness and my depression.

I missed the days when I was a single adult before this daughter of mine had found her way into my life. It was a carefree life, full of possibilities and with no responsibilities. I could go where my heart desired or see whatever friends I wanted to see. The world was open, and I could follow its call whenever the need arose. But I left this life behind too early and exchanged it for a cage of regret. All my friends had begun their careers and were ready to enjoy life, planning their future however they wished. I was left forgotten and alone, dreaming of being next to them in the photos they shared and videos posted.

It wasn't that I lacked in compassion or love for my daughter. On the contrary, I loved her very much. I just wasn't ready to raise someone else at such a young age. It had left me sad and alone; a broken soul without purpose or identity.

Who am I?

The question seemed lost in the busyness of raising my child. There was no time to understand who I was or who I wanted to be. Life was flying by and it left me feeling aged, old, and wrinkled. Nothing in my life was as I had wished it to be or dreamed of. My wings had been cut, and I came crashing down to earth to fall flat on my face.

But as I looked into my daughter's eyes, I could not help but smile through my tears. She was all I had and I was all she had. I would do anything for her.

Yet, the struggle remained as I stood wrestling with my soul. It was a struggle between my selfish desires and the love for my daughter. But who could fix this within me, this struggle that kept me from moving on in life?

There was this idea of God, but who was he to me? I was raised in a church, but those days were long gone. My daughter's birth became more important than a religion and searching for God on my own. For all I knew, God planned this to punish me and not because he loved me. I could see it in the eyes of my parents who judged me for what I had become. All I wanted was to be set free from my cage and to fly again like the days of my youth.

I needed help, but there was no one to turn to. Everything I tried made me empty and could not fulfill. Life felt real enough and trying to think of someone up in the sky showing me unconditional love didn't feel like the right answer.

But the constant tugging at my heart wouldn't stop.

I knew deep down how imperfect and incapable I was in leading someone else. This girl, this young girl that relied on me already caused my selfish desires to seep out from my very being. Hiding it now was impossible. Her tears streamed down her cheeks and dried on her shirt, and my sinful habits were the cause. How could I continue to raise her when my failures kept adding up?

How could I ever make it through?

I was exposed, vulnerable, and unable to hide my faults. Before my daughter was born, it was easy to only show my good side to others when the time was right, just the best part of who I was. Now, now my entire being was exposed. All of it: my insecurities, faults, and failures. Every part of my life that I didn't want to share was laid open by this child of mine. Everything she saw, every poor decision and hateful words, would be remembered as a lasting scar on her heart. What I saw was a selfish part of me that had lain in the shadows, hidden from the world and those around me. And I hated what I was because this little girl who I loved saw it all.

Yet, no matter my mistakes or how I tried to push her away in my sadness, she always came back. She never stopped following me and relied on me for her every need. She saw my failures but loved me still. Why was it not enough?

I do not know how or if I could conquer the selfishness and sorrow that encompassed my heart, no matter how hard I tried.

Would God know or even care? Did he understand how much of a stumbling block I was to my child? I am nothing close to the life that Jesus lived on this earth, and I missed the mark completely, unable to see and unable to understand how broken I truly was. But here I was and the one who had more faith in me was my daughter, standing by my side, unwilling to let go.

If she only knew!

If she only understood that I am an empty shell who would never amount to anything purposeful in this life. Yet, here I was. I had no choice; I had no option but to help her grow up and not make the same mistakes.

I wiped away the tears in my eyes as I bent my knees to give my daughter a hug. Her tears dried on my shirt as her hug was filled with pure love and innocence. She could not see my own tears that flowed silently onto her back. But I found the strength to finally lift her up and it was then that I realized she was holding something in her hand. As I moved to see what it was, I saw my small Bible held tightly between her small fingers. She must have picked it up on the small nightstand in my room. How she found it I do not know, but this had to be a sign from God.

For I knew, deep down, that I could not do this on my own any longer.

Faith I needed to find because faith is what this girl had in me.

THE SHOWER

It was always crowded where I lived and alone time was a treasure that could never be found. A small house with a big family is not a recipe for solace. This left me without a single room or corner to escape the pain and hardships of life with no interruption. And I needed this more so today than any other before. It was a day where no mask or makeup could cover the feelings that were kept inside. I needed it, desired it, craved it.

My only thoughts were to escape. I had to make it to my sanctuary where the only protection I knew awaited. The yelling followed close behind, reaching my ears without fail and making me cringe as if it came with another painful hit, a reaction that came too easily for me. I sought safety as quick as I could, running up the creaky old stairs that somehow withstood the test of time.

As long as I didn't hear another set of feet, I knew that my sanctuary would be reached without fail. The stairs protected me in this way, always bringing a warning of things to come, a foreboding of the inevitable. But not if I could lock myself into my sanctuary. It was only here that I knew everything would be well, at least for that short period of time.

As I made it to the top of the stairs, I grabbed the rail to change my direction as quick as I could. The door lay close enough down the hall, where safety felt real, and the yelling would finally be silent. Everything would become like a bad dream, a fading memory of a life that did not exist. My hands reached out, knowing that pushing the door open was simply to run into it as fast as possible. The wood pushed back against my palms as I hit it harder than usual, but it gave way all the same. I did not care much for the aching palms that had hit the door as it was nothing compared to the pain that wracked my entire body.

As soon as I found myself within the bathroom, I turned around to close the door as quick and hard as physically possible. I left nothing to chance; nothing would stop it from shutting. The only thing left was to turn the key for the lock and hope that it would hold up against any banging or pushing that would come its way.

The shower promised me a place of uninterrupted refuge that would cover the pain that I needed to let out. It beckoned my name, urging me to enter as quickly as possible. There was only time to remove my outer layering of clothes before I jumped into the shower. My body dropped to the shower floor in utter exhaustion. The initial shock of cold water covered my body before the mixture of warmth settled in. I needed the sound of the water to cover the sadness that my soul was trying to hold in since I came home.

Time passed slower as the water settled into its rhythmic flow. It mixed with my tears and flushed them away, away from the shaking and sobbing that had taken hold.

I did not know when the warmth of the hot water, which had flowed around my body and down the drain, ended its comfort to my soul. Only the cold, consistent, crashing remained with its unending force of will to remove the remaining heat it had once brought. The shivers that came on only masked the thoughts that raced through my mind. Though, moving from my place of sorrow was not an option. I had no strength, no will power to get out. The shower brought a place of isolation, a way to remove myself from the sorrows that the world so readily gifted me. It was easier to think about this than the bruises that wouldn't disappear or be ignored.

The cold water was easier to deal with, simpler to handle than what the alternative would be. There were no tears left to be cried, only numbness mixed in with the throbbing pains and wounds that would never heal and left its mark on my innermost being. This time felt worse than any before, a final cut to an unhealed wound. It had bled dry, bled through all my tears, through my shattered heart where no pieces were left to pick up. The coldness that remained matched the water that flowed around me. I knew not what I should do or how I should move on.

All my efforts to do the right thing, to obey when asked, to serve when needed, and leave when told, were never enough. Yet, faults were found, and reasons were made. The hits would come and its cruel vengeance with it.

How could I move on if this was what life brought? Was there such a thing as being good enough? Was crying out for love worth it when love would never come? Crying only brought more pain, but the solace of the shower would cover it up. Here, alone, was my place of refuge.

My life was a story of mistakes, tragedies, and heartbreak. Where did I go wrong and what did I do to deserve this? There could be no happy ending when my heart had no power to love again. The scars were too deep, too painful, too dark.

I pounded the back of my head against the tiles that lined the bathroom wall, hoping to remove the pain that had flowed from my broken heart and into my head. If only I could separate the two, I thought, it would end the pain that hurt me so.

I breathed a prayer to God to take away my pain, but all I heard was the pounding of the cold water that would not cease. Why would he not answer me? Did he not understand my pain, my hurt? Would he not rescue me from the life that he had given me?

I thought the tears were dried up, but they came again nonetheless, and I sobbed through the pain and hurt that surrounded my life. Would I have to resign myself to such a painful existence with no way out? I felt like giving up and giving in. No rescue would come for a wretch like me. The pounding of the cold water provided me no answer or resolution, but I knew this. Even so, the shower would be my comfort, my solace, and my tears.

The longing for the end of this life and eternity only increased with every drop that hit my body before falling into the drain below.

THE MILLSTONE

*Whoever causes one of these little ones who believe in me to
sin, it would be better for him to have a great millstone fastened
around his neck and to be drowned in the depth of the sea.*
-Matthew 18:6

The climb up the hill had taken all the strength I had. I could hear the waves crashing against the rocks below and smell the salty ocean breeze around me. The coolness of the air brought relief to my body. It was the final taste of relief that I would experience, and I still believed it was more than what I deserved.

I leaned against the millstone that I had rolled up the hill. It was large, heavy and made of chiseled stone. In it was all the sin, all the shame and guilt of causing those around me to stumble in their faith. I had found a passion, a gratification of leading others into sin and taking away their innocence. My mind had justified this as a way to teach them the ways of the world and how it worked. But the truth was that I wanted to pull others down to my level of depravity so I could feel better about my sin and worldly lifestyle. It was far from anything to do with the goodness of God as I was living for my own pleasures and desires.

It wasn't until I saw the consequences of my actions that I realized my errors. I had lived a lifestyle that was against God while still claiming to follow him, and then encouraged others to do the same. It had caused them to be led astray because of me instead of following Jesus. The images of their faces haunted my dreams and wouldn't let go. It was then I knew that this required me to pay the highest price for my sins and actions. The guilt was too great and it had come to take the shape of a millstone.

I knew the time had come to drop the millstone into the ocean's deep and to throw the guilt away from the actions of what I had done. Yet, I knew that this millstone was not enough to pay the debt. I had to throw myself off the cliff with it. The hole in the middle of the disc would allow for a rope to be tied around it and then looped around my neck.

It was about time I thought. The breeze had cooled me enough to think clearly and my breathing slowed down as I leaned against the millstone. This would be it, the last time that my dreams of guilt would haunt me. It would all be over soon and it is what I deserved. No one else could pay for the consequences of my actions but me, and I could only hope that it was enough. I didn't believe or think that

there was another way to fully pay for what I had done. My life was the only atonement I could give as nothing else I had was worth enough.

I pushed the millstone as close to the cliff face as I dared, and looked over the edge one last time. The wind was calm, and the sun shone bright in the afternoon sky. I did not deserve the type of day that it was, but it was a welcoming sight before I took the plunge below. It momentarily helped to take me away from my thoughts. A final reprieve; a final moment of peace.

I looked up to the heavens and prayed for God to have mercy on those I had caused to stumble. At least they would deserve mercy when I did not. I didn't want it anyway. I didn't need mercy and I was too ashamed to ask for it. It was time for me to pay the price, no one else could and no one else should. The millstone was my sin to carry and my sin to take to the grave. A deep and cold grave at the bottom of the ocean floor.

I moved the disc sideways with the hole facing the ocean to keep it steady as I prepared myself. I tied the rope through the hole of the millstone and looped it around my neck. The weight of the stone was too heavy to lift, but it didn't matter. Small or large, the effect would be the same once gravity pulled it to the ocean floor below. I knew that the sin I had to bear would cause any man to sink under its weight, and I was no different.

I turned the millstone once more to make it easier to roll over the cliff. One last push was all it would take before it fell off the cliff and took me with it. I could hear the ocean waves below, even with the millstone blocking my view. I steadied myself, prepared to pay for my sins, and ready to take the fall. I closed my eyes, took a deep breath, and pushed with all my might.

It must've been some poor luck on my end, but before the weight of the millstone could pull me with it, the rope got caught in a sharp crack at the edge of the cliff and snapped. I could hear as the millstone crashed into the ocean below, taking with it all the sin and shame that had added up over the many years.

"No, no, no!" I cried while falling to my knees. It wasn't supposed to be like this. I had to go with it, to pay for my sins. There was no other way and now it was all lost, gone to the bottom of the ocean floor and swallowed up by its deep and dark depths. I looked over the edge but could see nothing, no trace of the millstone or the rope that was attached to it.

I remained there, staring over the cliff and the crashing waves below and wondering what would happen next. It was then that I noticed someone grasping my shoulder, pulling me away from the edge and turning me around.

A man, dressed in white and shining brighter than the sun itself, stood next to me. He spoke in a compassionate voice, "I paid the price that you could not. Go, and sin no more," He began, "Your sins are forgiven by my blood."

"I didn't want your forgiveness." I cried out loud, "I don't deserve it." My head hung low, unable to look Jesus in the eye.

"I will turn all things meant for evil to good and I have much work for you to do. You are no longer condemned through my blood and the debt that was paid." Jesus bent down and wiped away the tears that had formed around my eyes. At that moment I felt his love, his care, even for a sinner such as I. There was nothing I could've given to deserve this second chance, but I knew it would require much of me, and it was a sacrifice that I was willing to make.

NO GREATER SIN

I cannot understand or comprehend beyond what I see.
My sin and shame are too great, too heavy for me,
Who can remove this weight which is too much to bear,
Who could show me compassion, love and care.

It is only when I stand still, take time and pause,
That I remember the lies, deceit, and pain that I cause.
I do not like my thoughts, not when I am quiet and can think,
I feel a deep sense of remorse, not cured by any person or shrink.

I want to leave my thoughts behind,
To bury them deep and out of my mind.
Yet, they linger, and sit there in my dreams,
I cannot get rid of them, not by any means.

It is always there, showing my imperfection,
And to know that I need constant correction.
But God gives me his love, mercy, forgiveness and grace,
And carries me in his loving embrace.

THE ANXIOUS HEART

*We are afflicted in every way, but not crushed; perplexed, but
not driven to despair; persecuted, but not forsaken; struck down,
but not destroyed; always carrying in the body the death of
Jesus, so that the life of Jesus may also be manifested in our
bodies.*
-2 Corinthians 4:8-10

The growing shadow of my body rippled through the current of the water, casting an image of the broken soul it held hostage. Unstable, wavering, and anxious. My body walked with a will of its own as I watch from above, trapped in a struggle for control. The steps are slow and thoughtless in the setting sun, moving mechanically in one direction with no end in sight.

An eerie quietness surrounds me as if the trees themselves do not want to disturb my anxious and troubled heart. Oh, how I wish that the wind would whisper its song, or the trees speak with their age-old wisdom. Yet, their voices remain quiet in anticipation of the night that comes with the setting sun. My shadow follows me with each movement, speaking only through its reflection on the water's edge. All that I have are my own thoughts which has become the prison that surrounds and keeps me wrapped in a blanket of emotions.

My heart has no rest, afflicted by the burdens of the mind. Yet, I have not been crushed by its weight.

My thoughts are full of worry and sorrow of things I cannot change. Yet, I have not felt complete despair. I feel alone in my pain that no medicine can heal, cutting to the core of my very being. Yet, I do not feel any mortal wound.

I do not know how to end the ache in my heart or control its anxious call. I yearn for a voice from God, but the only thing I feel is His peace in the silence of the setting sun, a peace that eludes my very being. One step follows the other in an endless cycle of motion, the weight of an unknown conclusion for my anxiety which keeps me as its hostage. I can only take one step at a time, not knowing who can help carry the burden that seems heavier than the ocean itself. I hold on to the promises of God as I cry silently for his help in my moment of need. I pray for the pain to go, for a drug to bring me the cure I require and put an end to these sleepless nights. All I want is for my anxious heart to be freed once again.

I carry this affliction with me, not knowing or understanding its purpose. It will not end, it will not leave, and it will not let me go. An answer for this burden I desire, and is what I want. It is comfort that I seek, but I cannot have. The only thing I can hold to is my faith. No matter the stress and heartache, it remains by my side. I hold on to the hope through the promises of God. This I believe and this is what will bring me through.

THE HOUSE (PART 5) – THE BASEMENT

The pain from having to tell my last girlfriend the news that she was not as important as Jesus meant that I was alone, once again. I knew it was the right thing to do, but the pain would not go away.

Ahh! The pain, that throbbing pain in my chest which many refer to as the heart. I couldn't live without it and yet, it always seemed to cause me more pain than anything else. I guess that's why they call it heartache. This hurt made me look for ways to self-medicate. I couldn't look Jesus in the eye, I felt too bad and too depressed, even though he held the answers I needed.

I knew that there was only one place of solace left for me to go, and that was to the basement. I had to get away, to find a place of comfort from all the pain. I wanted, no, I needed to go there, to my place of darkness. To bathe in it, to live in it, to make my home in its solitude. I refused to believe that there was another way in which I could make it through the day. The basement was where I had to go.

Before Jesus knew what was going on, I quickly unlocked the basement door and locked it again behind me. As I walked down the stairs, there was no light, but I didn't need it. It all felt too familiar to me, as if it had been a comforting home before Jesus moved in.

The darkness called for me as I moved deeper into the depths below and grew in strength with each step. As I reached the bottom floor. I quickly headed to my corner, to the darkest spot, where no light could come through the cracks in the door. Yes, I thought to myself, this was my place of comfort. Now, I could live in my depression and pain. The cycle was complete, I ended up back where I began, before Jesus tried to rescue me.

It was a sad story, a sparkle of hope, a sparkle of a supposed new life with Jesus, but it all brought me back to the beginning again. The irony, I thought. The belief that God could somehow change me. It couldn't be further from the truth. "Look where I am now?" I wanted to shout out to Jesus. "You couldn't help a poor soul like me because I am right back where I started." All Jesus had done was give me hope, but instead it pushed me further into a state of despair, and my soul couldn't be saved. My spiraling depression only pushed me further into darkness where no light could ever reach me again.

As my thoughts began to slowly wane in the silence of the basement, I realized that something wasn't the same as before. The basement was…different. The floor

seemed, warmer, to the touch and the darkness wasn't as strong like I remembered it. I couldn't understand the changes because the coolness of the floor and dampness of the room was something that I had always considered to be constant.

Then the oddest thing started to happen. The darkness in the basement began making way for a glowing light and it brought with it mixed emotions in my soul. Here's the weirdest thing, the light seemed to come from me as it grew in size. I tried to cover myself with a blanket, but it became useless after a while.

Did you know that only a little light in a dark place could light the entire room? Well, I didn't know that until this happened. I could see the darkness disappear. I mean, there wasn't much to see in my empty basement, but I could see the walls and stairs that led up to the door.

But how could I light emanate from me? I started to look closer at myself. The light was coming from my chest out of all places! As I unbuttoned my shirt, the light shone even brighter. It spread from my chest into the rest of my entire body, and I looked like a sitting torch! Yet, the feeling wasn't a burning sensation, but one of warmth.

As I look from my body back to the basement room, goosebumps covered my skin. It was plain as day, hidden from me when I initially came down, but now the light illuminated it so I could not make any mistake of what I saw. On the ground lay a cross, not a deep dark pit, but a cross. This couldn't be, I thought to myself. How did this come here? I knew for a fact that no etching of a cross was in the basement when I first moved in. As my mind began to whirl, it turned my world upside down. The deep dark basement was supposed to be a place of comfort from the world, but it had already been invaded by Jesus! It is as if the foundation of my house itself was changed without my knowledge. It was no longer like the dark basement room that I once had.

I didn't know what to do, but I couldn't stay in the basement any longer, especially after this weird light that was beaming out of me like some sort of lighthouse to a wary sailor. I glanced up the stairs to the locked door. I had a sick feeling in my stomach that Jesus was probably standing behind it, smiling at the thought of my basement being full of light. I may as well go upstairs to speak with him about it. I slowly climbed the steps to the top. Even though the time seemed to take just as long to walk up as it did to walk down, the lighted stairs that came from me was still an odd sight to behold and made it easier to see where my feet was stepping.

As I unlocked the door, my suspicions were correct. There was Jesus, all smiles on his face, as if he was waiting to give me a big bear hug. He wanted to ask me what I thought about the new cornerstone that he had laid down on my floor. In order to move in, he began, it required for me to have a different foundation. He had done the groundwork from the onset, but never told me. I must've missed that part of the contract, just like everything else I wasn't ready for.

Jesus also explained that the light that came from my heart was the Holy Spirit and together with the two of them, I would never have to live in that dark place ever again. The new life did not stop me from experiencing pain, or hurt, or trials of many kinds, but he wanted me to know that with him, I would overcome it. I had been pulled out of the pit of darkness, and even though I may want to go back there at times, Jesus said that he would never leave me or forsake me. That meant he would never move out or leave me alone. I was more ready for this now than before.

I was redeemed from my sins, but I hadn't fully understood what it meant until now. My actions brought me to where I was and my actions against Jesus led to the hurt and pain in my house. I realized that, now with all the doors unlocked, it would be harder to hide anything from Jesus. Though, I kind of felt some relief from this. It was like I didn't have to perform well to be loved and that through Jesus' help and his great patience with me, I would eventually become more like him. It was crazy to think that I could change or that this life really meant a transformation, but I could see it better now than before.

This pain, this hurt I felt that brought me to the basement helped me see clearly of why I needed Jesus and why I had to rely on him when experiencing my pain and heartache. It wouldn't be easy in this life, but I think that, or I know that, I could make it through if I relied on his help. He wouldn't move out, and I had comfort in that.

After all that I went through, I would much rather have Jesus in my house than without. Oh my, I thought to myself, how things had changed. Before I wanted to kick Jesus out when he got involved in simple affairs. Now I wanted him to stay and get involved. Maybe this is what being born again truly meant. That I was a new person and my old habits and old ways had to die. I felt almost free, like the shackles were removed, and I could move on with my life.

Nothing would be easy, I knew this. Pain and loneliness I would feel at times; yet, with Jesus, I had all the strength I needed to get through it all. And my house was becoming like a magnificent mansion, much bigger and better than it had ever been before.

THE EMPTY BOTTLE

My thumb moved slowly down from the smooth glass of the bottle to rub against the texture of the paper. The movement had become a habit as I could feel and read the wrapper of the now empty bottle. The weight of the glass felt heavy, even after the contents had long since disappeared. As I sat on the sidewalk, a slight rain began to fall from the clouds above. The raindrops gave no relief as it would not fill the contents of the empty bottle in my hand. Instead it began to cleanse the haze that clouded my mind. I refused to move to a dry place, nor would I release the bottle, as it held more meaning to my life than it should. It was my very last possession besides the clothes on my back.

The drops covering the outside did not change the contents of the bottle. Its dryness showed no signs life, not even one last drop to taste. There was this unquenchable thirst that would never leave me. I longed for another sip, another taste, another minute of respite from the demons that tormented me. Instead of fulfilling my childhood dreams, the world only offered cruelty and unkindness. It refused to give me what I needed, and instead it only increased my thirst. I wanted to stand up and throw the bottle against the building behind, but there was no strength left in me to do so.

I couldn't hide from this place where I found myself; to forget all that brought me here. Yet, my home was the dark streets with the smells and dampness that represented the outcasts of society. I had to drown it all out somehow, and alcohol had once provided this temporary relief.

Regret, remorse, and relapse were the thoughts that clouded my mind and brought me to this point in time.

The regret for not keeping the promises I made.

The remorse for my failures and constant lying.

The relapse for falling back into my old ways and habits.

Who would show me pity now? At first I had made my way through life by asking for favors from family and friends to get better, and I truly believed that I could stop drinking when the time was right, but that never came. Each time I ran out, I found myself wanting just one more bottle, one more drink to quench my thirst. They didn't understand how these demons in my soul would torture me if I couldn't calm their voices. I had to have more.

When promising to get better didn't work anymore, I began lying about how I was better and I would say anything that made them feel pity for me once more. Nothing I said bothered me anymore as long as there was some money in their outstretched hand which allowed me to buy another bottle. It was after this that the worst part came, and that was the stealing. It wasn't noticeable in the beginning, but once I got bolder in what I took and sold for money I lost all sense of regret. My closest friends and family eventually found out, and I was cast out and banished. I had burned all relationships I had and was left with nothing; no place to stay, no money, and the hardest part, no alcohol to satisfy the demons in my head. I was truly an outcast with not a bed to lay my head.

I had failed everyone for the last time. The last chance was gone, I just knew it. I couldn't look anyone in the eye, not after having let them down. As I sat on the sidewalk with cars driving by, and the bottle still within the grasp of my hand, I realized how miserable I had become. I used to make fun of people who were homeless and alcoholics, never thinking that I would be one of them. Yet, here I was, an example of bad decisions to anyone passing by.

The only friend I knew, the only friend that could help and bring a cure for my misery was the same bottle that got me here to begin with. It brought the poison, but it also gave me the cure that I sought. The irony of the situation didn't stop me from believing the deception of relief and freedom. My pain was real and my medication had to be immediate. This was the quickest solution, the quickest way to forgetting everything.

The bottle…

Yes, the empty bottle that my thumb wouldn't stop moving across. It had run dry, I remembered it clearly. My thoughts started to focus again and anger overwhelmed me. The promise of respite that it gave was only temporary. It lied to me and it made my feelings of pain even greater. The cure that it asked for was that I just had to get more. Yet, I could not move. My hand clenched the bottle, but it refused to respond to my thoughts. I was stuck in a never-ending trap with no way out.

My reflection appeared on the bottle as I looked into it. I couldn't see much, but what I did, I did not like. It was a poor sight indeed. Is this what I have become? Is this all that I am good for in this pain-filled world?

In the back of my mind, I knew what I had to do; to find a solution for my addiction. But I didn't think there would be any hope left for me or strength to do it. Failure is too painful, and alcohol is ever crouching at the door to consume me. Its promises never fulfilled and would never do so, I knew. The whispers that filled my head would find me no matter how far I tried to run away.

The sound of the church bell brought me out of my own thoughts. It was louder than I imagined and the shock caused me to drop the bottle to cover my ears. The ringing of the church bell left me paralyzed and I couldn't hear the sound of the bottle breaking apart on the asphalt below. As the final toll came, I looked up and behind me. The church tower stood tall as it rang its bell at the stroke of midnight. I must've sat down next to the church without realizing it.

As my eyes focused on the church itself, a breeze caused the door to slightly swing open, inviting me into its sanctuary. There was little left keeping me out on the streets. If only for a place to sleep at night, it would be a welcome respite. I left my place on the sidewalk, forgetting the broken bottle that lay shattered by my feet, and moved towards the entrance of the doors.

I knew little of this Jesus person, but even after entering into the sanctuary, I could begin feeling less thirsty and a peace surrounding me that I never experienced before.

ROCK BOTTOM

My eyelids struggled to open, refusing to respond to my call. It felt like pushing on an unused and rusty door.

Something wasn't right, but what?

It didn't help that my thoughts were cloudy, unclear, and unable to comprehend my current predicament. Nothing about my body spoke of having a restful night's sleep and trying to move around required more effort than usual. My senses began to overwhelm my thoughts, sending me information faster than I could digest. Each one brought me a different part of the whole, giving me details of where I was: The rhythmic and beeping sound of the heart monitor, the feeling of dry and unused lips begging for water, needles in my arm, straps holding me still, and the smell of cleaning chemicals that would make a normal person gag. Each carried a hint and confirmation of where I had woken up.

The reality of my predicament started to sink in, and my mind began to fight for attention and time to analyze the new information of my surroundings. Did I ever imagine waking up in a hospital bed or find myself in a place of healing? I tried licking my lips, blinking my eyes, and moving my body, hoping to gain more clarity and awareness. I did not remember the moments leading up to losing consciousness. Thinking about it only brought a headache that pushed me from accessing the distant memories held captive by my body's painful reaction.

I just wanted to drift back to sleep and forget everything; to believe it was all a nightmare that would end once I truly woke up.

How had my life come to this point? The question seemed more rhetorical than I wished it to be. It was clear what brought me to this…this predicament. I just thought that it wouldn't come to this, that it wouldn't be me who ended up on a hospital bed.

I refused to acknowledge that my decisions would ever lead to these consequences.

Me?

Never!

I was too young and mentally tough; too headstrong and self-disciplined. Too…wise.

These feelings of euphoria were meant to be temporary, nothing that would've lasted as long as it did. That first decision to take the drugs was to forget about the reality and rules, fit in with my friends, and to find an escape, ignoring the consequences that consistent use would bring. The thought that my actions, my spiraling addiction, would bring me here never crossed my mind. I had hit rock bottom and the guilt brought tears to my eyes.

The tears didn't last long because it couldn't have been all my fault. I looked for someone or something to blame for why my life had come to this conclusion. The pain in my heart grasped onto the first image, that of my parents. They pushed me to find solace in drugs, to escape from their controlling behavior and strict rules. If they had been more loving and let me do what I wanted, then it would not have led to my rebellious behavior. Yes, it was their fault I thought to myself, their failures and decisions brought me to this point.

Yet, something didn't feel right. Could they truly be blamed for my behavior? They tried to care for me, to help me see the consequences of my actions, but I would not listen. I had pushed them away like I did everyone else. All that remained was the drugs and all it left me was pain and emptiness. Nothing could fill the hole that grew deep in my heart. The silence of the room was deafening. The only thing that remained was the rhythmic beeping of the heart monitor. It never showed sympathy nor care to the suffering of my pitiful existence.

I turned my eyes to the ceiling. Wondering, waiting for when my life would end. All I had was gone and it left me lonely and sad. The drugs were not there to give me the comfort that I once had. I knew that life gave no second chances, but I wished for one more, nonetheless. To go back in time with the wisdom I had gained from my experiences and try to do better. I knew things would've turned out differently. But it was too late for that now. Everything was lost and when I got out, the drugs would come calling for me once more.

Yet, a doubt crept slowly into my mind. Maybe they still loved me? Maybe…I thought, they would forgive me one last time for my faults and failures. I didn't deserve it one bit, not after what I had done. The thoughts quickly turned negative. My consequences were real, and forgiveness would not be possible. And just like life, my friends and family would not give me a second chance.

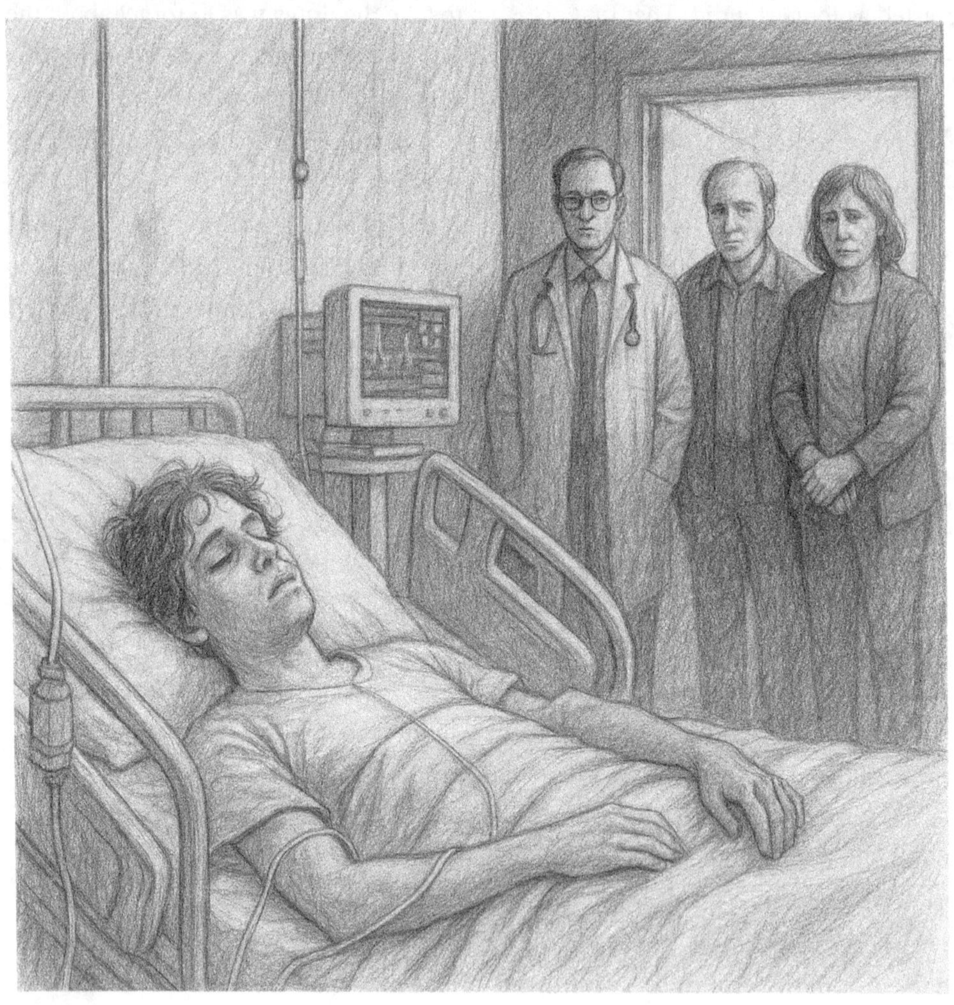

I had sunk to the bottom of the ocean, out of breath and out of hope. There was no place left where I could go, and I had no idea where to begin. Was life worth it to keep going on? I didn't know and I didn't much care. Maybe God would listen and grant me a wish to start over, but this was too much to ask, even for Him.

I let out a "heh!" as a relief for the comedic thoughts of redemption that had entered my mind. My soul was too far gone for anyone to care or to take pity on me. I felt my eyelids begin to close as staying awake left me with little strength. Maybe a miracle would happen, but I doubted it. Life was too harsh for someone like me. I welcomed the sleep as it draped over my eyes and stopped my mind from thinking any more than it had already.

The door opened and the doctor stepped into the room. Behind him stood a couple, eyes full of compassion and care for their lost child, waiting…hoping…praying.

THE GLOCK

The weight of the Glock in my hand felt familiar. It was barely used, but had been part of my life for as long as I remember. The metal was cool to the touch as I ran my fingers across the contours of the gun. No matter all the things going on around me, this weapon was always the same, unchanging through the years. It had only one more duty to carry out before I would let it go.

As I racked the slide to load a new round, I could hear the smoothness of the metal moving, fully lubricated and clean, as if it was never used prior to this point in time. I held the Glock in my right hand, as I tried to envision the bullet sitting in the chamber of the gun, ready to spring into action. My fingers slowly set itself into place. No longer was the gun a simple metal object, it was cocked and loaded, ready to fire a deadly projectile in whatever direction I willed it.

The Glock had a heaviness to it as I sat on my chair, contemplating what I had done in my life. My story was one full of bad decisions followed by the wrong type of consequences. I had no skills in my life to use and I was out of ideas on what I needed to do. I had chosen work over school and friends over my kids. Now everything had come crashing down. My children hate me and my job was lost. There was nothing left to live for. My knees were ruined from years of work, and there was no insurance to cover the surgeries required. It was painful to even walk. Who would want to take care of me now? What kind of job could I even find? I was dependent on social welfare and an outcast of society.

My future was as bleak as it could be and there was nothing left to live for. It would be better to end my life now than to continue on like this for as long as my body held together. Pulling the trigger on this gun seemed a much easier solution and a better way out than what stood in front of me. There was nothing good but a final resting place six feet underground.

For too long I have been sitting around the house without any energy or ability to be of use. I did not want to be a burden to everyone around or ask for help. My

wife left me long ago and is already doing better without me as I had failed to be a part of my children's lives. The opportunity to set an example for my son and be a father to my daughter had disappeared long ago. What do they even think of me now? They must be wishing for a different dad than the one they got in me. Even my ex-wife must have regretted marrying me. I believe this and it has to be true. My life was worthless and finished.

My thoughts brought me deeper into depression as the liquor continued to pump through my body after a full night of drinking. It brought all the negativity out from the darkness of my soul and told me how much of a failure I am. The gun began to feel warm in my grip, asking to be used, asking to be the solution that I craved. I know it would not be long before this miserable life would end. No one would shed a tear for me, not one soul in this cursed life.

I lifted the gun up to my head, hoping for a quick death as I closed my eyes. The pressure of the trigger could be felt as my finger slowly curled inward. The click would come any second and the world will soon have one less soul to worry about and believed it was the right thing to do. One final breath of air filled my lungs and then the pressure of the trigger gave way…but nothing happened. I took the gun down from my head and looked at it. The safety was still on as my heart beat a hundred miles an hour. I forgot to remove the safety. I took a deep breath and with a moment of clarity beginning to set in, I realized how close I had been to taking my very life. Doubt started to creep in as I wondered if it was the right decision after all. The alcohol had brought a moment of weakness that had almost left me lifeless.

As my thoughts clouded my judgement, the phone beeped on the table next to me. The sound was distinct and one that I had grown very used too. I put the gun down on my bed and lifted up my phone. The message was short and clear, and somehow warmed my heart and soul. The sudden thought of almost taking my very life shocked me and left me in tears. How could I leave this life before saying goodbye to those I love?

The text message was very simple, yet profound. I stared at it for what seemed like forever.

It read, "Jesus loves you, dad."

GIVE UP

Give up!

There it was again, that voice inside my head. Even now, it wouldn't stop with its singular message, having grown louder upon each negative experience or thought that this life brought my way. It was easy to brush off at first, but just like an ever-beating gong, its efforts were not in vain. The mental blocks broke down and it left me vulnerable to its simple message. The voice was always the same; never encouraging, never thoughtful, and never caring. Its purpose and plan meant to bring relief for my struggles by telling me that it wasn't worth it anymore; that giving up was an easy way out, and the right one. But deep down, I knew its cure would bring an irreversible and final ending to this wretched existence.

Give up!

It always came; always found its way back from the recesses of my mind. The moments of sadness and depression were never far away and like a boomerang, they would come back just as fast as when they left me. And that voice would always play itself in my most vulnerable state. It kept me from find a way out and instead it pulled me deeper into its dark waters where lightness disappeared and breathing seemed impossible. It whispered its words into my ears and then shouted it when I refused to take the action it wanted me to take…until I did. It wanted…no, it demanded that I heed its message.

Give up!

I couldn't tell when these feelings all began. It seemed as if it was always a part of me, always there, burying itself deep inside until slowly it started to find its way to the surface. It wasn't long before the world became a dark and dreary place. No one truly understood how I felt. Its message made up who I was. I just couldn't make the voice stop as it pushed me off the ledge I once stood upon.

Give up!

The worse I felt, the more power it had over me. It left me ashamed, broken, and naked. I pushed those who loved me away because my pain should not become their pain. They should be protected from me and the failures that surrounded my life. It was because no matter how hard I tried, I would always be useless and a waste of space to everyone around. My existence was really this pointless. The voice agreed with my feelings, and its solution was simple. Its cure called me to action, and I had finally answered.

Give up!

The blood from the cuts on my wrists were pulsating like the seconds on a clock. I looked down in defeat, knowing that I had truly given in and given up. This life would soon end and everyone would be happy and move on without me. I began to feel tired and my thoughts weren't as clear as before. Regret and the fear of total darkness began to set in. A moment of fear brought me back from collapse as my adrenaline kicked in. "What have I done?"

Give up!

The voice tried to push away my doubts, unwilling to let go of its grip and hold over my life decisions. How could I dwell in a sea of darkness and allow this voice to speak its command into my life? It had no purpose but death, no gift but poison. And I had taken what it offered. Staying here, I could not. I had to get out and seek help. Yet, this cave, this darkness was a comfort from the pain, a relapse into my brokenness. I just needed someone to come, to be an answer of prayer, to save me, and to let me know that life was still worth living.

Give up!

This was not me any longer, I knew this. The emotions welled up and I began to cry, letting out all my pain while unable to get up or move to seek help. I had to escape from the dungeon of my depression. I hadn't tried praying before, but I thought it was worth a try. "Dear God," I cried in my tears and sorrow, "I don't know if you're real or listening, but if you are, please save me from this wretched life. I cannot do this any longer." Silence was my reply, and I do not know if it worked. Time was quickly running out, even if I didn't want it to. If there was a savior, he would have heard and answered my plea. The adrenaline ran its course, and my eyes grew tired once again. It wouldn't be long now.

As I struggled to hold up my head, I could barely recognize knocking at my door. "Don't give up!" the voice said, "we're here and we love you!"

I couldn't respond, it was too difficult to do and sleep was quickly approaching. Maybe, I thought to myself, this was the beginning of a new life? If I could only hold on for a bit longer.

"Don't give up." The irony of that statement brought a smile to my face. Yes, this was the voice I needed, and the encouragement I required.

UNTIL DEATH

It was an odd thing to know the timing of your own death. It is never truly how you envision it.

"You should never have come here!"

"Where is your god now?! Can he save you?"

"Why don't you pray more!"

"Liar!"

"There is no god!"

The voices from the crowd tore at my soul as the guards pulled me through the mass of people that had gathered around. There wasn't much that I could do but feebly cover my face as people spit on me and threw rocks from all different kinds of angles. It was my fault, there was no denying that. I had stirred up the anger of the people to a tipping point, having pushed beyond my limits by preaching about Jesus to the wrong crowd. It was at that moment the chief of police got involved and everything happened faster than I had imagined. Before I had a chance to defend myself, I was convicted of blasphemy and preaching a false religion with a punishment of death by hanging.

I looked up to see the gallows fast approaching. The guards made a way, but the crowd wanted their words, bitterness, and anger to be released in order to satisfy their appetite for justice. All I could do was mourn for their lost souls and try my best not to react in a negative way. It was what I knew to do best.

Sadness filled my soul. It wasn't just for the people of the town, but also for what I had gotten myself into. I didn't want my life on earth to end this quickly and this early. Yes, I knew what awaited me in heaven, but that didn't change the reality of my life on earth. All the friendships and family that I loved and who I couldn't say goodbye to were not here with me. If I had only known that this would

be happening, then it would be easier. But, would I have gone to this country anyway? The conflict between following God's will and the human nature for comfort and happiness tore at my soul.

The thoughts continued to flash through my mind, and I barely noticed that my guards had already led me up the steps to the platform above. It wouldn't be long now.

I never thought my last time in front of people would be in silence. It was always to preach the gospel message as it was what I loved to tell people about the most. Though, this time, the

crowd cheered for different reasons, and it wasn't for hearing the good news of the Bible. Neither would there be any last words or goodbyes to give. This was taken from me.

I'm used to a rowdy crowd, preaching to the lost always left a few angry and unrepentant souls, but never did I see myself having to face a punishment for crimes that were based their hatred of the gospel. It was not true justice, but an unfair and cruel injustice.

How can they be so against what Jesus came to do, even to the point of murder? I only preached what would save their souls, but instead they rejected the message, rejected Jesus, and ultimately blamed me for their problems. I had become the focus of their anger; disrupting their society and hurting those who held power.

Did I make a wrong decision to come here? The thoughts sifted through my mind as I tried to block out the noise around me. I was always quick to preach and never took calculated decisions in reaching the lost. People had warned me that I should be more careful, to not offend certain officers within the cities I went to. I never cared much for these warnings. If I had not gone, then who would have? My focus was to preach the gospel and believe that God would protect me through all the trials that would come my way, even if death would be the ultimate sacrifice.

Yet, here I was, at the end of my road and ministry journey. There were no regrets, only sadness that I couldn't reach more people in my short time on this earth. The wood creaked below my feet as it was ready to swallow my soul, reminding me how short this life is to those who do not have an eternal home waiting.

I could feel the rope around my neck as it held me in place. The strings that were bound together swayed in the wind, ready to do its singular purpose. Facing death isn't easy, but at the same time, I knew that this life was temporary. It didn't stop me from wondering if maybe God still had work for me to do and if a last-minute rescue would happen. Was my work on this earth really done? I felt I had so much more to give. Sadness for those around me only grew with each passing minute.

Neigh, I could not forget, I could not hold those thoughts in my mind. This may be my end, but God knew best. This I had to believe. I changed the lives of many during my time on earth and I knew that the work of God will carry on. It was not the end, just the end for me on this earth. I looked forward to heaven and the glory that I would see and wondering if God would consider me a good and faithful servant?

Yet, fear still filled my mind and would until death. Doubt of my decisions kept me from being focused. I closed my eyes briefly. I could not see nor did I want to see the end that stood in front of me. There was no place to run, no place to go. I had to face the music. My only comfort was that my savior suffered worse and died for me, and he had bought me with the price of his blood. There was no turning back.

As the executioner was ready to pull the lever to the trap door below, I looked out amongst the crowd one last time. It was then that my eyes noticed something familiar. I quickly focused my eyes on what I thought was an imagination. Yes, it was truly them! My three closest disciples were there, holding up hands in prayer to God over my soul. A tear streamed down my face, not just for my loss in discipling them, but also because God had prepared a path for those who would walk where my steps had ended. Peace flooded through my soul, knowing that God was truly in control, even here, even now.

TRUE CHARACTER

Our true character, our true nature
Deceives those we have come to know
Hiding in the dark recesses of our soul
Waiting, watching, to escape its fragile cage

Our thoughts are chained to its will
Churning our minds to its deceiving call
We struggle to show only our noble side
Straining to contain it with a forced smile

Its voice echoes inside, crying to be set free
And when we grow weak, we give in for all to see
Releasing it from the dark to cloud the light
Shattering the myth of our fictional selves

Perfection has been lost and hypocrisy gained
Our sin and shame tell us to run away, to hide
We desperately try and rebuild the crumbling wall
Sending us back into the blackness we know so well

Only a glimmer of hope, a ray of light that stops us
It shines through our darkness in the shape of a cross
Telling us that there is a better side, a better way
If only we will cry out for what has been freely given.

Father, forgive us for we have sinned,
Let your true character and glory shine through us!

FINDING INNER TRANQUILITY

Can we seek and find a place of solitude and inner tranquility?
Where would you look, where should you go? Is it somewhere in your vicinity?

In the busyness of life, we forget what it means to lay down and relax.
We let the day go by so fast, rushing around as if our capacity is at max.
We have no time for God, no time to forget about the stresses of life.
Can we not just find joy in the day we have without the constant strife?

The commandments that God gives to help us is not a priority anymore.
Where's the time with our creator? Do we really love him at our very core?
We cry out for anyone to give us the meaning for the time we spend on work.
Can this be all that life is meant to be, waiting for the next useless bonus or perk?

There has to be a way, a method, to remove the stress from our body and mind.
A sanctuary to give us peace so we can lay down, close our eyes, and unwind.
If only we understood that God created the Sabbath for us to abide in his rest.
He gave us the time we need for worship and praise; to remember we are blest.
Do not fret, worry, or let the empty idols from this material world take control.
God is always here, ready to take over so he can free you by saving your soul.

So go to a quiet place and shut off the outside world for a minute or two.
Close your eyes and do not let any distractions come through.
Remove any noise that makes its way into your ears.
So that God can take away those troubles and fears.

Stand still and listen, let God play a beautiful melody that will continually grow.
Breathe in and out and make a day for rest so that God's abiding love can flow.

SPRINTING TOWARDS THE GOAL

*But one thing I do: forgetting what lies behind and straining
forward to what lies ahead, I press on toward the goal for the
prize of the upward call of God in Christ Jesus.*
-Philippians 3:13-14

I stand,
Perplexed by your continuous calling of my name.
Refusing to give up as I hide behind my anger and shame
I have found no meaning from the path of my own choosing
And it was only your voice during this time that was so soothing
I grew to resent the road that I had chosen over the years
Wishing that I could take back the time I had spent in tears
As I stand, it is your love that has finally captured my heart
Pulling me towards yourself and the joy that you impart.

I walk,
Being drawn slowly toward you each day and night
Even with the worldly pleasures so close, I keep trying to find your light.
Walking takes every ounce of energy as I continuously lose focus on my goal
And when I feel like giving up, it is you who covers and fills my life-sized hole
My walk is not straight and I still stumble in my sin as I try to stay on your path
In my self-pity, you remind me to look on your Son who covers me from wrath
And I have learned to see you through the fog of my short life on this earth
So I walk, not by my will, but yours, as I hear you tell me how much I'm worth.

I run,
The trials that you have helped me overcome have given me renewed joy
I see the chains of the past falling away with each link you break and destroy
The rust was there and all I had to do was entrust it all to you
As I was molded to be free and to see things from your worldview
You have changed me, loved me, disciplined me, and led me through the flame.
And I run to draw nearer to you, as I see that you have loved me all the same.
You're the one that has the faith in me when it should be the other way around.
And as I see your Son on that cross, I praise you for letting grace abound.

I sprint,
So that I will not be entangled by everything that I have left behind me.
It is from these things in my life that I have learned to refuse and flee
Your promises of a new birth and new life have given me the joy to carry on
You are my everything and I know you will be there when all else is gone
I can barely fathom the depth of your love and mercy for me, which is infinite
I do not want to experience the emptiness again without you, even for a minute
I will never stop sprinting towards you, oh Lord
And the goal of eternal life that you have given me, my reward.

MY DEVOTION

In all my pain, my sorrow, and my sadness Lord, my heart remains steadfast. I sing with joy because you are the only thing I can hold onto. Everything else that I tried to worship could never last and it never satisfied. I have sacrificed time with you and your will in pursuit of idols that took my utmost devotion. But you bring me back Lord, as you have always done, and I cannot stop praising you for your faithfulness.

You are my shepherd and you call to me as one of your own. I hear your calming voice and it breaks the chains that bind me. You are my heart, my devotion, and my love. I will remain steadfast Lord because your love for me is higher than the heavens and your faithfulness to me reaches to the skies. I will praise you to the nations and exalt your name among its people. Oh Lord, let your name be glorified through me so that others may see and believe.

My Lord, I pray that you will provide help in my time of persecution. The times when I cannot stand without your aid. That you will deliver me as you have promised and done before. That when I am drowning in a deep, dark sea, I can reach for your caring hand. Please do not reject me in my time of need.

When I am drowning in a deep, dark sea, I can reach for your caring hand. The human idols I have put my trust in before will not deliver me as they failed to do in the past. Human effort for salvation is worthless and bring no lasting comfort or joy.

Only with you, Lord, will I gain victory over my enemies. It is you that will trample on Satan's plans and deliver me. It is your hand that will direct my path. Thank you, Lord, for loving me. I will praise you and sing of your victories forevermore.

Biography

Stefan Johnsson currently resides in Houston, TX where he lives with his family. He grew up in the mission field of Sweden, having parents who worked with immigrants and refugees. As someone who is passionate about society, he found himself pursuing Sociology and History as majors at the University of Kansas. He later studied at Webster University in their Global Master's in International Relations.

Stefan is also a technical and professional writer, focusing on helping foreign professionals succeed in their pursuit for work in the U.S. He is a proud member of the Every Nation church network and is the editor for his home church's daily devotional blog. Having grown up in different cultures, Stefan is constantly looking to question how we, as Christians, can better serve those whom we interact with in our communities and to be a light for the kingdom of God. He is passionate about writing and has published several books including *Wise Words from the Word* and *Breaking Barriers*.

You can follow him on Instagram (@StefanJ_Author) or on Goodreads.